Les Femmes Savantes

Les Femmes Savantes

Molière

Translated by Richard Wilbur
Annotations by Richard Williamson

HIPPOCRENE BOOKS
New York

This edition is published in the United States of America by Hippocrene Books
in 1997 by arrangement with Harcourt Brace & Company.
For information, address:
Hippocrene Books, Inc.
171 Madison Avenue
New York, NY 10016

Library of Congress Cataloging-in-Publication Data
Molière, 1622-1673
[Femmes savantes. English & French]
Les femmes Savantes / Molière
p.   cm.
Text in English and French, with critical matter in English.
Includes bibliographical references.
ISBN 0-7818-0398-5
I. Title.
PQ1833.A475   1996
842'.4—dc20   96-30108
CIP
Printed in the United States of America.

Contents

Molière: A Theatrical Life

During the fourth performance of *Le Malade Imaginaire* on the evening of 17 February 1673, Molière began to vomit blood forcing him to leave the theater of the Palais-Royal. Soon after, he died in his nearby residence, on the Rue de Richelieu, at the age of fifty-one. Because Molière had failed to renounce his life as an actor on his deathbed, Louis XIV appealed to the archbishop of Paris, Monseigneur de Horlay, to allow his favorite and famous dramatist to receive a Christian burial. The archbishop granted the King's request—reluctantly—for the Catholic Church believed that all actors in their ability to assume different identities were disciples of Satan. Molière was thus buried at nine in the evening on 21 February 1673 in the Saint-Joseph cemetery, normally reserved for unbaptized children. In spite of the archbishop's desire to keep the ceremony low-key, over eight hundred people, including the well-known poet and friend of Molière, Nicolas Boileau, attended the funeral.

The detailed and precise account of Molière's final days is an anomaly in our current knowledge of his life. No letters, no personal autobiography, no *mémoires,* no manuscripts, no original documents belonging to the great dramatist have yet been discovered by the hundreds of biographers and critics who have devoted their lives to helping us better understand the man and his work. Indeed, his life, or what we know of it, is composed of "maybes," and has faded into the legend of the "*Grand Siècle*" of Louis XIV and into the glory of Molière's theatrical legacy: thirty-four plays. Much like the work of an equally enigmatic playwright, William Shakespeare, Molière's comedies continue to inspire audiences throughout the world and remain as relevant and as funny to us now as they were to Parisian theatergoers in the middle decades of the seventeenth century.

Although we are unsure of the exact date of his birth, Jean Poquelin was baptized in the Eglise Saint-Eustache on 15 January 1622. Named after his father, a prosperous rug merchant living on the Rue St-Honoré in Paris, Jean added a "Baptiste" to his name when a brother was also baptized "Jean" in 1624. Marie Cressé, his mother, died when Jean-Baptiste was only ten years old, and his stepmother, Catherine Fleurette, died in 1636, thus leaving Jean Poquelin with the arduous task of earning a living and raising five children. Spending much of his time with his grandfathers, Jean-Baptiste may have attended some performances of the *farceurs* in the Hôtel de Bourgogne, a well-known theater of the time. He may have seen the *commedia dell-arte* with its stock characters playing common roles, its rapid pace, and its heavy use of physical gags to create laughter.

To be sure, the young Poquelin was introduced to classical theater in the prescribed curriculum of study in the Collège de Clermont, which he attended from 1633 to 1639. The Jesuit teachers required students to read and write Latin (the only language spoken in the Collège); to study ancient rhetoric and the canonical works of Greek and Latin literature, including the plays of Aristophanes and Euripides; to analyze the texts of Aristotle; and to develop habits of intellectual rigor and curiosity.

Sometime between the end of his schooling in the Collège de Clermont and the beginning of law studies in Orléans, Jean-Baptiste may have met the Epicurean philosopher, Pierre Gassendi, and become a member of his circle of *libre-penseurs*, or "free-thinkers," those who sought philosophical truth outside the dogma of the Catholic Church. This encounter would have a subtle and diffuse influence on Poquelin's future work. But another encounter during these same years would mark a definitive and profound change of direction in the young man's life.

We don't know exactly when they met or how—perhaps they were neighbors in Paris—but the relationship between Madeleine Béjart and Jean-Baptiste was crucial in steering the young lawyer away from a career in law, or even thinking of taking over the rug business from his father. Instead, he now aimed for an illustrious life in the theater. Four years older than Poquelin, Madeleine Béjart was an aspiring and talented actress with an intimate knowledge of the contemporary French stage. Her beauty and her professionalism must have been sufficient to seduce the young lawyer to become an actor. Much contrary to the wishes of his father, he signed the founding agreement of the *Illustre Théâtre* on 16 June 1643. From that moment to his death, the biography of Jean-Baptiste Poquelin is transformed into the legend of Molière, a pseudonym he assumed early in 1644.

Molière's first experience in a theater company was quite unfortunate: in August 1644, he was thrown into the Châtelet prison for unpaid debts. Because Paris had only a few theaters, all occupied by successful troupes, the Béjart family, Molière, and the other founding members of the *Illustre Théâtre* had to sink borrowed money into the renovation of an old squash court, *Les Métayers*, to stage their plays. They then needed to buy costumes, materials to construct stage sets, and even large candles to provide lighting. Recognizing his considerable talent in facing the challenges of inaugurating a new theater, the principals and actors of the *Illustre Théâtre* elected Molière to be director of the company. Thus, when the performances did not bring in enough money to pay the creditors, it was Molière, the director, who was imprisoned. Freed on bail provided by a friend of the troupe, Molière must have then realized that a life in the theater would require hard work, abundant energy, and money. Whatever may have been his thoughts after that rude beginning, he persevered and was determined to succeed. However, before triumphing on a Paris stage, Molière and his colleagues spent a long and difficult apprenticeship of some thirteen years in the French provinces.

It was not unusual for theater troupes to travel from city to city to present plays, much like a circus or a carnival show today. Through tedious examination of archival documents it is now possible to sketch out Molière's peregrinations: Nantes and Rennes (1645); Toulouse and Carcassonne (1647); Nantes again (1648); Narbonne (1649-1650); Grenoble and Lyon (1652); Montpellier (1653-1654); Lyon again (1655); Avignon (1657); and finally, Rouen. Wherever he traveled, Molière brought the soothing balm of laughter to people menaced by famine, epidemic, and warfare. The troupe's repertory consisted primarily of farces in the tradition of the Italian *commedia dell-arte*, with an occasional tragedy. Fortunately, Molière succeeded in attracting the patronage of several influential and wealthy patricians, such as the Duc d'Eperon and the Prince de Conti, who provided much needed financial and moral support to the dramatists. In addition to honing his skills as an actor and director and learning how to handle the various responsibilities of running a theater company, Molière probably wrote his first plays, *L'Etourdi* and *Le Dépit amoureux*, both farces, during this extended tour of provincial cities.

When the *Illustre Théâtre* was performing in Rouen during the summer of 1658, Madeleine Béjart journeyed to Paris to explore the possibility of re-establishing the troupe in the capital. She returned to Rouen with an eighteen-month lease on a converted squash court in the Marais section. And through the political connections Molière had formed with the Prince de Conti and others, the king's young brother decided to place the troupe under his protection and to make them *Comédiens de Monsieur*. With renewed enthusiasm and considerable seasoning, Molière, Madeleine, and the other ten comedians of the *Illustre Théâtre* prepared to act on a Paris stage for the first time in over thirteen years.

Because of the success of the troupe in the Marais theater, the young Louis XIV and his brother asked Molière to perform in the Louvre Palace on 24 October 1658. Although the director chose to present *Nicomède*, a tragedy by a well-known playwright, Pierre Corneille, he added a short farce to the program, which made the king break into hearty laughter and convinced him to give Molière the opportunity to share the *Petit-Bourbon* theater, one of the most well-equipped and luxurious in Paris, with an Italian troupe. Performing on Mondays, Wednesdays, Thursdays, and Saturdays, Molière enjoyed ample time to watch the Italian comedians on the other nights of the week and to grow more familiar with the different plots and techniques of the *commedia dell-arte*. He also must have realized that the Parisian theater public was ready for a new type of comedy. On 18 November 1659, following again a tragedy by Pierre Corneille, *Cinna*, Molière presented a play he had written himself, *Les Précieuses ridicules*. It was such a triumph that the price of seats doubled for subsequent performances, and the king supposedly saw the play several times.

Success, of course, brought fame and prestige to Molière and his troupe: people buzzed in the literary salons and in Louis's court about this funny farce that dared to satirize the excessive and pretentious refinement of some well-to-do ladies. But success also created petty jealousy among rival dramatists, who recognized in this author, actor, director, and stage manager, talents they lacked. In addition to writing and directing plays, a time-consuming challenge to be sure, Molière would now need to devote much of his energy to combat critics, competitors, and even those who tried to publish pirated editions of his plays. Fortunately, his indefatigable ambition to succeed in a difficult enterprise did not diminish, and he continued to weather attacks on his personal and professional life.

After the success of *Sganarelle ou le cocu imaginaire* in May 1660, and the relative failure of *Dom Garcie de Navarre*, a tragi-comedy, performed in the new theater of the Palais-Royal (February 1661), Molière wrote a play that proved his genius in combining certain elements of both farce and tragedy to create a new kind of comedy, one that appealed directly to the tastes and needs of his audience, and to us. *L'Ecole des maris* (24 June 1661) makes us laugh but also provokes us to reflect upon our social and human condition: *castigat ridendo mores*. So impressed by the play and Molière's growing reputation was Fouquet, the director of finances for Louis XIV, that he asked Molière to write and stage a play at the celebration of the completion of the Château de Vaux. With his uncanny ability to write quickly and appropriately for the circumstance, in under two weeks Molière produced a new genre of play, a ballet-comedy, *Les Fâcheux*, which combines text, dance, and music.

1662 was a momentous year for the great author. In February he married Armande Béjart, the sister of Madeleine and twenty years younger than Molière. (This difference in age has led some biographers and critics to claim that Armande is the daughter of Molière and Madeleine, but again this is another improbable "maybe" in his life.) The marriage to an attractive woman so much younger than he may have reinforced a popular theme in his plays: *le cocu imaginaire*, for he did suffer from jealousy and feared that he might lose Armande to another man.

Then, in December, he gave the premiere of *L'Ecole des femmes*, his seventh comedy and the first five-act play he had written in alexandrine verse. Its success can be attributed not only to box office receipts, but to the scandal it provoked. Those who had been dismayed by Molière's popularity were waiting impatiently for a pretext to attack him. Even with the generous financial support of the king, Molière was compelled this time to respond to his detractors. Two plays, *La Critique de "L'Ecole des Femmes"* (June 1663) and *L'Impromptu de Versailles* (October 1663), gave Molière an opportunity to poke fun at his enemies and to explain how difficult it can be to make people laugh. To the critics who accused him of not following the sacrosanct dramatic conventions of the period, he responded in the voice of Dorante: "*Je voudrais bien savoir si la grande règle de toutes les règles n'est pas de plaire, et si une pièce de théâtre qui a attrapé son but n'a pas suivi un bon chemin*" *(La Critique,* Scene VI*).*[1]

Although the *querelle*, or debate, finally subsided after almost two years, Molière's enemies were not about to relinquish their attack. When Molière presented *Le Tartuffe ou l'Hypocrite* in May, 1664, before the king and his entourage, including Cardinal Chigi, the Pope's ambassador to the Royal Court, it did not take long for Molière's detractors to regroup, joined this time by the mysterious and powerful Compagnie du Saint-Sacrement. Swayed by the loud outrage and political influence of the devout members of the Compagnie, the king forbade any more public presentations of *Le Tartuffe*. But, as we can perhaps judge from Molière's long sojourn in the French provinces and his reaction to the *querelle* of *L'Ecole des femmes*, he did not give up easily. Indeed, he rewrote certain parts of the play and waited for a more propitious moment to stage it: 5 February 1669. Between this temporary defeat and resounding success, Molière wrote thirteen plays, including his most memorable and well-known: *Dom Juan, Le Misanthrope, Le Médecin malgré lui,* and *L'Avare.* And his troupe was now truly an illustrious one, for in 1665 Louis XIV named it the *Troupe du Roi* and granted it a generous subsidy.

---

1 "I'd like to know if the most important rule of all is not to please, and if a play has done that, then it has succeeded."

In their new role as personal theater company of Louis XIV, Molière and his comedians were expected to provide frequent *divertissements du Roi*, or festivals, at the Royal Court. After suffering a bad case of pneumonia (probably), which prevented him from acting and shut down his theater for a year (1665-1666), Molière authored six comedies in one year, many of them, such as *George Dandin* and *Monsieur de Pourceaugnac*, to be staged at Versailles or at Chambord to amuse the king. For instance, in the cadre of the *divertissement royal* in 1670, he collaborated with the French musician, Jean-Baptiste Lully, to create an extravagant ballet-comedy, much applauded by members of Louis's court and by the king himself, who had dictated the subject of the play, *Les Amants magnifiques*, to the playwright and had even expected to dance in one of the ballets (fearful of losing his dignity, the king decided against it).

However, as occupied as he must have been in writing and producing these *divertissements*, Molière did not neglect his faithful and admiring theater public in Paris. He presented *L'Avare* at the Palais-Royal in 1668, one of his most popular plays today and one of the few five-act comedies he wrote in prose. And, of course, he finally succeeded in staging *Le Tartuffe ou l'Imposteur*, which was such a theatrical event that Molière, in the role of Orgon, had to act even on the evening of his father's death. He also brought to Paris some of the plays he had staged first for the king. Created in October, 1670 as a *divertissement du Roi*, *Le Bourgeois gentilhomme* was an immediate success at the Palais-Royal a month later. Its comical portrait of an ignorant bourgeois, Monsieur Jourdain, who sets out to learn everything, but must begin with the pronunciation of the five vowels, continues to appeal to French audiences and is often on the program of the "*Comédie-Française*" (the recording group performing the French play on accompanying audio cassettes), itself the legacy of the *Troupe du Roi*.

Increasing ill health? Diminishing energy and enthusiasm? Marital difficulties with Armande? Whatever may have been the reason, Molière only staged two productions in 1671: the tragedy-ballet, *Psyché*, again in collaboration with Lully, and the rather dark comedy,

Les Fourberies de Scapin. Nonetheless, he had been working diligently on two plays, *Les Femmes savantes,* presented on 11 March 1672, only three weeks after the death of Madeleine Béjart, his professional and personal companion since the founding of the *Illustre Théâtre* in 1643. Finally, on February 10, 1673, after some thirty years of a life devoted to the theater, Molière staged his last play, *Le Malade imaginaire,* which some critics, including André Gide, hail as a *chef-d'oeuvre.* Playing Argan, who thinks he is quite sick, is the truly ill Molière who will die soon after the fourth performance of the play. Both are acutely aware that illness may, indeed, result in death and that doctors with their obscure Latinate expressions and all the medicines they prescribe can offer only temporary relief, if any, to the human condition. In *Le Malade imaginaire,* as in the other plays of Molière, we understand and appreciate more profoundly Victor Hugo's pertinent phrase: "Laughter is the sun that drives winter from the human face." Molière's comic wisdom has enriched us for over three centuries.

Introduction to Les Femmes savantes

In writing and in staging *Les Femmes savantes*, Molière was inspired by two contemporary events: a long-standing, smoldering dispute with l'abbé Cotin and the widespread popularity of feminine literary salons.

L'abbé Cotin, almost seventy-years old by the first performance of the play on 11 March 1672, was an influential figure at the Royal Court and a member of the prestigious Académie française. He had riled Molière by his virulent and relentless attack on *L'Ecole des femmes* in 1662, citing the play as immoral and irreligious. In an acerbic pamphlet circulated in 1666, *Critique désintéressée sur les satires du temps*, l'abbé Cotin condemned all actors as partners of the Devil (the Catholic Church's viewpoint at the time) and made thinly veiled references to Molière and his troupe. And in 1668, he attacked Nicolas Boileau, Molière's friend and fellow combattant in the never-ceasing war of words that sought to both discredit Molière in the king's favor and to chase him from the Paris stage. We can explain Molière's biting satire of Trissotin (or "triple sot," three-times-a-fool), a pedantic and worthless literary hack, as a delightful way of revenging l'abbé Cotin's numerous personal attacks on him. To assure that the Parisian theater public recognized the real person in the character of Trissotin, Molière even uses one of l'abbé Cotin's poems in the third act, where the "learned ladies," Armande, Bélise, and Philaminte, listen in ecstasy to Trissotin's reading of the sonnet.

With her frequent comments supporting a formal education for women, and with her desire to create an "academy" of the arts and sciences solely for females, Philaminte represents the growing number of women, mostly aristocratic, who peopled literary salons and insisted upon gaining equality with men. Indeed, the numerous salons, such as the one presided over by Madeleine de Scudéry (1601-1677), presented a context for discussing not only recent novels, poems, or plays, but also for debating the kind and purpose of education appropriate for women. This debate, known as the *querelle des femmes*, had been occurring since the late Middle Ages, but intensified in the middle decades of seventeenth-century France. In the character of Philaminte, Molière seeks to mock those upper middle-class women who would aspire to salon life; he satirizes less those who seek a better education for women than those whose learning is superficial and ostentatious. As Voltaire wrote to Madame du Châtelet, a most "learned lady" indeed, in the dedication of *L'Alzire* (1736):

> Mais Molière, ce législateur dans la morale et dans les
> bienséances du monde, n'a pas assurément prétendu, en
> attaquant les femmes savantes, se moquer de la science et de
> l'esprit. Il n'en a joué que l'abus et l'affectation.

In his first great theatrical success, *Les Précieuses ridicules* (1659), Molière had poked fun at preciosity—a fastidious over-refinement in language and manners. In *Les Femmes savantes* he satirizes preciosity once again, but the real target is Philaminte's monomaniacal devotion to discussing philosophy and to developing plans for her "academy." Her desire for personal glory plunges her family into conflict and perturbs the bourgeois order of seventeenth-century France, in which the authority of the father is predominant and unquestioned.

Les Femmes savantes takes place in the home of Chrysale, a well-to-do member of the upper middle class. By qualifying him as a *bon bourgeois* in the cast of characters, Molière signals to his audience that this family is **not** aristocratic, that it should conform to certain social conventions, and that Philaminte's pretensions to great learning are really a thinly-veiled attempt to seek higher social status. One such convention dictates that Henriette, the younger daughter, cannot wed Clitandre, the man whom she loves and who loves her, without the approval of her parents. Armande, perhaps because of jealousy (Clitandre had once courted her), perhaps because of petty self-interest, implores her sister not to marry at all: who would want to be responsible for a husband, for children, for running a household? Armande prefers a spiritual, platonic attachment to the baseness of physical love. The merry and witty Henriette responds by asking her sister where they would be now if their mother had refused physical contact with their father. In this opening confrontation between Henriette and Armande, Molière succeeds in presenting two conceptions of a woman's role in society: the traditional (love-marriage-family) and the liberated (refusal to accept the patriarchal order). His creation of a sympathetic Henriette suggests that he favors the traditional and finds Armande's conception quite unnatural.

Clitandre and Henriette believe that they will have no problem in obtaining the consent of Chrysale, but Philaminte may indeed create a challenge: she is enraptured by Monsieur Trissotin. Although Clitandre is unaware that Trissotin will soon become his rival, he paints an unflattering, even vicious, portrait of this pedant. We can imagine Molière's delight in throwing a few sharp barbs at l'abbé Cotin so early in the play.

The first act ends in a hilarious encounter between Clitandre and Bélise, Chrysale's old-maid sister. Even though the young man insists that he loves Henriette, Bélise is persuaded that he truly burns to possess her, and willingly misinterprets everything he says to her. Bélise's purposeful blindness forewarns us of Philaminte's folly.

In many of Molière's plays, the plot hinges on convincing a father to allow his daughter to wed the man who loves her. At the beginning of Act II of *Les Femmes savantes*, Chrysale quickly approves the marriage of Henriette to Clitandre and presents no obstacle to their happiness. Normally, approval by the father would suffice in a bourgeois family, but not in this household. Indeed, Martine rushes in to tell her master that Philaminte has dismissed her. And when Philaminte arrives to explain her action, we can see that Chrysale is a hen-pecked, pusillanimous husband easily dominated by his wife, a situation that Molière's public must have considered unusual and unnatural. We see also the extent of Philaminte's pedantic preciosity: she has fired her servant for uttering **one** uncouth word. In one of the longest tirades in a Molière play, Chrysale criticizes women who neglect their household duties to study astronomy or write poetry:

> Il n'est pas honnête, et pour beaucoup de causes,
> Qu'une femme étudie et sache tant de choses.
> *—II, 7*

These two lines have often been pulled out of context to prove that Molière suffered from an advanced case of misogyny. Chrysale does suggest that Philaminte and other *femmes savantes* have gone too far in their devotion to learning and have lost a sense of balance. However, as will become clearer in the play, Molière satirizes pseudo-intellectuality and cannot be criticized as anti-intellectual or absolutely against the education of women. Coming from an idle bourgeois who uses his volume of Plutarch to press his collars, Chrysale's denunciation of the "learned ladies" sounds hollow.

After Philaminte announces her irrevocable decision to marry her daughter to Trissotin, Ariste encourages Chrysale to regain the upper hand in the household, for in his mind it is inappropriate that the wife assume control. Obviously, given Chrysale's weakness and Philaminte's determination to have her way, Henriette is in big trouble. She can only hope that it is possible to re-establish the authority of her father.

Much like Tartuffe in Molière's famous play, Trissotin does not appear on stage until the third act. Before that point, we have learned much about him and know how thoroughly he has seduced Philaminte and gained her favor. In the presence of the three *femmes savantes*, Armande, Bélise, and Philaminte, Trissotin recites two of his most recent poems. A contagious and comic infatuation seizes the women and they repeat each line with cries of ecstasy or merely utter sighs of rapture. What renders them funny in the ensuing conversation is their shallow, artificial intellectualism: they can speak the correct terms of philosophy, of astronomy, and of physics; they know the proper names to cite, like Descartes and Epicure; but they do not truly understand these disciplines. Finally, their egotistical belief that they alone will be arbiters of correct "language" manifests a selfish desire for power for its own sake:

> Nul n'aura de l'esprit hors nous et nos amis.
> —*III, 2*

Trissotin is briefly unmasked during a loud dispute with Vadius (another hack writer). Ordinarily reserved and polite, he becomes unruly and crass, thus revealing his true nature: a scheming, greedy, petty writer of inconsequential texts—not the great author the "learned ladies" have worshipped. Nonetheless, Philaminte adheres to her resolve and officially announces Henriette's betrothal to Trissotin.

In the fourth act, the two rivals finally meet but not before Philaminte has again expressed her determination to prevail in the power struggle with her husband. Trissotin reveals to Clitandre that he desperately needs to marry a rich women: his writings provide only a meager income. Clitandre attempts to point out to Philaminte Trissotin's superficial grasp of knowledge and his greediness, but her own follies render her blind to the truth. Not even the receipt of an anonymous letter (probably from Trissotin's rival, Vadius) detailing Trissotin's plagiarism of classical authors can convince her to change her mind. When she sends for a notary to draw up a marriage contract, Clitandre and Henriette fall into deep despair and Henriette promises her lover that she would rather enter a convent than marry Trissotin.

With the notary on his way to the house the fifth act opens with a discussion between Henriette and Trissotin: she uses her considerable tact and charm to dissuade him from the marriage, with no success. As all are assembled, even Chrysale who has tried to shore up his courage once again to confront his wife, the notary begins the contract. Suddenly, Ariste appears with two letters, one for Philaminte and the other for Chrysale. Philaminte has lost a trial and must pay a large sum. Chrysale learns that the two bankers to whom he had entrusted almost all his money have declared bankruptcy. Thus informed of the family's unfortunate financial disaster, Trissotin begs out of the wedding. Philaminte then realizes how she has been cruelly duped by this greedy poet:

Qu'il a bien découvert son âme mercenaire!
Et que peu philosophe est ce qu'il vient de faire!
—*V, 4*

And she quickly consents to Clitandre's demand for her daughter's hand. Happily, Ariste had invented these two letters as the only way of unmasking Trissotin and forcing Philaminte to regain her senses. The last two lines of the play suggest that the family has re-discovered its equilibrium, or, at least, that Chrysale has re-assumed the power he had lost to his wife. In a forceful and authoritative voice, he now commands the notary to draw up a new wedding contract:

Allons, monsieur, suivez l'ordre que j'ai prescrit,
Et faites le contrat ainsi que je l'ai dit.
—*V, 4*

Molière's audience in the Palais-Royal must have greeted this happy ending with relief. Thanks to Ariste's *deux ex machina* use of letters to unmask the hypocrite and to bring Philaminte's reign of terror to an end, a more natural order has been re-established, at least in the view of the Parisian public of 1672. Of course in modern society our sensibilities have changed dramatically; in France, the United States, and other countries, women enjoy many more opportunities for self-realization than in seventeenth-century France. Nonetheless, *Les Femmes savantes* remains particularly contemporary and meaningful. Does not the debate on the proper role of women in society continue in full force? Are there not those, like Chrysale and Henriette, who admonish women to remain at home to raise children, and those who criticize this traditional role? While we may laugh at Philaminte's firing of Martine for saying an uncouth word, does not the "tyranny of words" still exist in its present form of "politically correct" speech? And in our present-day society where young people are often criticized for their rudeness and disrespect, are not the good manners, common sense, and self-control of Henriette and Clitandre refreshing and admirable? Finally, in her drive to obtain personal glory and power, Philaminte illustrates for us the unfortunate results of extremism. In Molière's world, radical views create blindness and folly. As Philinte says in *Le Misanthrope,*

La parfaite raison fuit toute extrémité.
—*I, 1*

In the closing years of the twentieth century, we need to laugh at such folly, and be wary of it.

Les Femmes savantes

PERSONNAGES

CHRYSALE	bon bourgeois
PHILAMINTE	femme de Chrysale
ARMANDE	fille de Chrysale et de Philaminte
HENRIETTE	fille de Chrysale et de Philaminte
ARISTE	frère de Chrysale
BÉLISE	soeur de Chrysale
CLITANDRE	amant d'Henriette
TRISSOTIN	bel esprit
VADIUS	savant
MARTINE	servante de cuisine
LEPINE	laquais
JULIUS	valet de Vadius
LA NOTAIRE	

La scène est à Paris

CHARACTERS

CHRYSALE	a well-to-do bourgeois
PHILAMINTE	Chrysale's wife
ARMANDE	daughter of Chrysale and Philaminte
HENRIETTE	daughter of Chrysale and Philaminte
ARISTE	Chrysale's brother
BÉLISE	Chrysale's sister
CLITANDRE	Henriette's suitor
TRISSOTIN	a wit
VADIUS	a scholar
MARTINE	kitchen-maid
LÉPINE	a servant
JULIEN	valet to Vadius
A NOTARY	

The scene: *Chrysale's house in Paris*

Act I

Scène Première

ARMANDE

Quoi! le beau nom de fille[1] est un titre, ma soeur,
Dont vous voulez quitter la charmante douceur,
Et de vous marier vou osez faire fête[2]?
Ce vulgaire[3] dessein vous peut monter en tête?

HENRIETTE

Oui, ma soeur.

ARMANDE

   Ah! ce oui se peut-il supporter?
Et sans un mal de coeur[4] saurait-on l'écouter?

HENRIETTE

Qu'a donc le mariage en soi qui vous oblige,
Ma soeur...

ARMANDE

   Ah! mon Dieu, fi!

HENRIETTE

    Comment?

Scene One

ARMANDE, HENRIETTE

ARMANDE

What, Sister! Are you truly of a mind
To leave your precious maidenhood behind,
And give yourself in marriage to a man?
Can you be harboring such a vulgar plan?

HENRIETTE

Yes, Sister.

ARMANDE

Yes, you say! When have I heard
So odious and sickening a word?

HENRIETTE

Why does the thought of marriage so repel you?

ARMANDE

Fie, fie! For shame!

HENRIETTE

But what—

ARMANDE

Ah! fi! vous dis-je,
Ne concevez-vous point ce que, dès qu'on l'entend,
Un tel mot à l'esprit offre de dégoûtant[5],
De quelle étrange image on est par lui blessée,
Sur quelle sale vue il traîne la pensée?
N'en frisonnez-vous point? et pouvez-vous, ma soeur,
Aux suites de ce mot résoudre[6] votre coeur?

HENRIETTE

Les suites de ce mot, quand je les envisage,
Me font voir un mari, des enfants, un ménage;
Et je ne vois rien là, si j'en puis raisonner,
Qui blesse la pensée et fasse frisonner.

ARMANDE

De tels attachements[7], ô ciel! sont pour vous plaire!

HENRIETTE

Et qu'est-ce qu'à mon age on a de mieux à faire,
Que d'attacher à soi, par le titre d'époux,
Un homme qui vous aime et soi t'aimé de vous,
Et de cette union, de tendresse suivie,
Se faire les douceurs d'une innocente vie?
Ce noeud bien assorti[8] n'a-t-il pas des appas[9]?

ARMANDE

Mon Dieu, que votre esprit est d'un étage[10] bas!
Que vous jouez au monde un petit personnage,
De vous claquemurer[11] aux choses du ménage,
Et de n'entrevoir point de plaisirs plus touchants
Qu'un idole[12] d'époux et des marmots[13] d'enfants!
Laissez aux gens grossiers, aux personnes vulgaires,

ARMANDE

For shame, I tell you!
Can you deny what sordid scenes are brought
To the mind's eye by that distasteful thought,
What coarse, degrading images arise,
What shocking things it makes one visualize?
Do you not shudder, Sister, and grow pale
At what this thought you're thinking would entail?

HENRIETTE

It would entail, as I conceive it, one
Husband, some children, and a house to run;
In all of which, it may as well be said,
I find no cause for loathing or for dread.

ARMANDE

Alas! Such bondage truly appeals to you?

HENRIETTE

At my young age, what better could I do
Than join myself in wedded harmony
To one I love, and who in turn loves me,
And through the deepening bond of man and wife
Enjoy a blameless and contented life?
Does such a union offer no attractions?

ARMANDE

Oh dear, you crave such squalid satisfactions!
How can you choose to play a petty role,
Dull and domestic, and content your soul
With joys no loftier than keeping house
And raising brats, and pampering a spouse?
Let common natures, vulgarity inclined,

29

Les bas amusements[14] de ces sortes d'affaires.
A de plus hauts objets élevez vos désirs,
Songez à prendre un goût[15] des plus nobles plaisirs,
Et, traitant de mépris[16] les sens et la matière,
A l'esprit, comme nous, donnez-vous tout entière:
Vous avez notre mère en exemple à vos yeux,
Que du nom de savante on honore en tous lieux;
Tâchez, ainsi que moi, de vous montrer sa fille,
Aspirez aux clartés[17] qui sont dans la famille,
Et vous rendez[18] sensible aux charmantes douceurs
Que l'amour de l'étude épanche dans les coeurs.
Loin d'être aux lois d'un homme en esclave asservie,
Mariez-vous, ma soeur, à la philosophie,
Qui nous monte au-dessus de tout le genre humain
Et donne à la raison l'empire[19] souverain,
Soumettant à ses lois la partie animale,
Dont l'appétit grossier aux bêtes nous ravale[20].
Ce sont là les beaux feux[21], les doux attachements,
Qui doivent de la vie occuper les moments;
Et les soins où je vois tant de femmes sensibles
Me paraissent aux yeux[22] des pauvretés horribles.

HENRIETTE

Le ciel, dont nous voyons que l'ordre est tout puissant,
Pour différents emplois nous fabrique en naissant;
Et tout esprit n'est pas composé d'une étoffe
Qui se trouve taillée à faire un philosophe.
Si le vôtre est né aux élévations[23]
Où montent des savants les spéculations,
Le mien est fait, ma soeur, pour aller terre à terre,
Et dans les petits soins son faible se resserre.
Ne troublons point du ciel les justes règlements
Et de nos deux instincts suivons les mouvements.

Concern themselves with trifles of that kind.
Aspire to nobler objects, seek to attain
To keener joys upon a higher plane,
And, scorning gross material things as naught,
Devote yourself, as we have done, to thought.
We have a mother to whom all pay honor
For erudition; model yourself upon her;
Yes, prove yourself her daughter, as I have done,
Join in the quest for truth that she's begun,
And learn how love of study can impart
A sweet enlargement to the mind and heart.
Why marry, and be the slave of him you wed?
Be married to philosophy instead,
Which lifts us up above mankind, and gives
All power to reason's pure imperatives,
Thus rendering our bestial natures tame
And mastering those lusts which lead to shame.
A love of reason, a passion for the truth,
Should quite suffice one's heart in age or youth,
And I am moved to pity when I note
On what low objects certain women dote.

HENRIETTE

But Heaven, in its wise omnipotence,
Endows us all with differing gifts and bents,
And all souls are not fashioned, I'm afraid,
Of the stuff of which philosophers are made.
If yours was born for soaring to the heights
Of learning, and for speculative flights,
My own weak spirit, Sister, has from birth
Clung to the homelier pleasures of the earth.
Let's not oppose what Heaven has decreed,
But simply follow where our instincts lead.

Habitez, par l'essor d'un grand et beau génie[24],
Les hautes régions de la philosophie,
Tandis que mon esprit, se tenant ici-bas,
Goûtera de l'hymen[25] les terrestres appas.
Ainsi, dans nos desseins l'une à l'autre contraire,
Nous saurons toutes deux imiter notre mère:
Vous, du côté de l'âme et des nobles désirs,
Moi, du côté des sens et des grossiers plaisirs;
Vous, aux productions[26] d'esprit et de lumière,
Moi, dans celles, ma soeur, qui sont de la matière.

ARMANDE

Quand sur une personne on prétend se régler,
C'est par les beaux cotés qu'il lui faut ressembler,
Et ce n'est point du tout la prendre pour modèle,
Ma soeur, que de tousser et de cracher comme elle.

HENRIETTE

Mais vous ne seriez pas ce dont vous vous vantez
Si ma mère n'eût eu que de ces beaux côtés;
Et bien vous prend[27], ma soeur, que son noble génie
N'ait pas vaqué[28] toujours à la philosophie.
De grâce, souffrez-moi[29], par un peu de bonté,
Des bassesses à qui vous devez la clarté[30],
Et ne supprimez point, voulant qu'on vous seconde,
Quelque petit savant qui veut venir au monde.

ARMANDE

Je vois que votre esprit ne peut être guéri
Du fol entêtement de vous faire[31] un mari;
Mais sachons, s'il vous plaît, qui vous songez à prendre.
Votre visée au moins n'est pas mise à Clitandre?

You, through the towering genius you possess,
Shall dwell in philosophic loftiness,
While my prosaic nature, here below,
Shall taste such joys as marriage can bestow.
Thus, though our lives contrast with one another,
We each shall emulate our worthy mother—
You, in your quest for rational excellence,
I, in the less refined delights of sense;
You, in conceptions lofty and ethereal,
I, in conceptions rather more material.

ARMANDE

Sister, the person whom one emulates
Ought to be followed for her finer traits.
If someone's worthy to be copied, it's
Not for the way in which she coughs and spits.

HENRIETTE

You and your intellect would not be here
If Mother's traits had all been fine, my dear,
And it's most fortunate for you that she
Was not wed solely to philosophy.
Relent, and tolerate in me, I pray,
That urge through which you saw the light of day,
And do not bid me be like you, and scorn
The hopes of some small scholar to be born.

ARMANDE

Your mind, I see, is stupidly contrary,
And won't give up its stubborn wish to marry.
But tell me, do, of this intended match:
Surely it's not Clitandre you aim to catch?

HENRIETTE

Et par quelle raison n'y serait-elle pas?
Manque-t-il de mérite? est-ce un choix qui soit bas?

ARMANDE

Non; mais c'est un dessein qui serait malhonnête[32]
Que de vouloir d'une autre enlever la conquête:
Et ce n'est pas un fait dans le monde ignoré
Que Clitandre ait pour moi hautement[33] soupiré.

HENRIETTE

Oui; mais tous ces soupirs chez vous sont choses veines,
Et vous ne tombez pas aux bassesses humaines:
Votre esprit à l'hymen renonce pour toujours,
Et la philosophie a toutes vos amours.
Ainsi, n'ayant au coeur nul dessein pour Clitandre,
Que vous importe-t-il qu'on y puisse prétendre?

ARMANDE

Cet empire que tient la raison sur les sens
Ne fait pas renoncer aux douceurs des encens:
Et l'on peut pour époux refuser un mérite[34]
Que pour adorateur on veut bien à sa suite.

HENRIETTE

Je n'ai pas empêché qu'à vos perfections
Il n'ait continué ses adorations,
Et je n'ai fait que prendre, au refus de votre âme,
Ce qu'est venu m'offrir l'hommage de sa flamme.

HENRIETTE

Why not? Of what defects could one accuse him?
Would I be vulgar if I were to choose him?

ARMANDE

No. But I don't think much of your design
To lure away a devotee of mine;
Clitandre, as the world well knows, has sighed
And yearned for me, and sought me as his bride.

HENRIETTE

Yes; but such sighs, arising as they do
From base affections, are as naught to you;
Marriage is something you have risen above,
And fair philosophy has all your love.
Since, then, Clitandre isn't necessary
To your well-being, may he and I not marry?

ARMANDE

Though reason bids us shun the baits of sense,
We still may take delight in compliments;
We may refuse a man, yet be desirous
That still he pay us homage, and admire us.

HENRIETTE

I never sought to make him discontinue
His worship of the noble soul that's in you;
But once you had refused him, I felt free
To take the love which he then offered me.

ARMANDE

Mais à l'offre des voeux d'un amant dépité
Trouvez-vous, je vous prie, entière sûreté?
Croyez-vous pour vos yeux sa passion bien forte,
Et qu'en son coeur pour moi tout flamme soit morte?

HENRIETTE

Il me le dit, ma soeur, et, pour moi, je le croi[35].

ARMANDE

Ne soyez pas, ma soeur, d'une si bonne foi[36],
Et croyez, quand il dit qu'il me quitte et vous aime,
Qu'il n'y songe pas bien et se trompe lui-même.

HENRIETTE

Je ne sais; mais enfin, si c'est votre plaisir,
Il nous est bien aisé de nous en éclaircir.
Je l'aperçois qui vient, et sur cette matière
Il pourra nous donner une pleine lumière.

ARMANDE

When a rejected suitor, full of spite,
Claims to adore you, can you trust him quite?
Do you really think he loves you? Are you persuaded
That his intense desire for me has faded?

HENRIETTE

Yes, Sister, I believe it; he's told me so.

ARMANDE

Sister, you're gullible; as you should know,
His talk of leaving me and loving you
Is self-deceptive bluster, and quite untrue.

HENRIETTE

Perhaps; however, Sister, if you'd care
To learn with me the facts of this affair,
I see Clitandre coming; I'm sure, my dear,
That if we ask, he'll make his feelings clear.

Scène II

CLITANDRE, ARMANDE, HENRIETTE

———————————

HENRIETTE

Pour me tirer d'un doute où me jette ma soeur,
Entre elle et moi, Clitandre, expliquez votre coeur,
Découvrez-en le fond, et nous daignez[37] apprendre
Qui de nous à vos voeux est en droit de prétendre.

ARMANDE

Non, non, je ne veux point à votre passion
Imposer la rigueur d'une explication:
Je ménage les gens et sais comme[38] embarrasse
Le contraignant effort de ces aveux en face.

CLITANDRE (à Armande)

Non, madame[39], mon coeur, qui dissimule peu,
Ne sent nulle contrainte à faire un libre aveu;
Dans aucun embarras un tel pas[40] ne me jette,
Et j'avouerai tout haut, d'une âme franche et nette,
Que les tendres liens où je suis arrêté,
    (Montrant Henriette)
Mon amour et mes voeux, sont tout de ce côté.
Qu'à nulle émotion cet aveu ne vous porte:
Vous avez bien voulu les choses de la sorte.
Vos attraits m'avaient pris, et mes tendres soupirs
Vous ont assez prouvé l'ardeur de mes désirs;

Scene Two

CLITANDRE, ARMANDE, HENRIETTE

HENRIETTE

My sister has me in uncertainties
As to your heart's affections. If you please,
Clitandre, tell us where your feelings lie,
And which of us may claim you—she or I.

ARMANDE

No, I'll not join in making you reveal
So publicly the passion which you feel;
You are, I'm sure, reluctant to confess
Your private feelings under such duress.

CLITANDRE (*To Armande*)

Madam, my heart, unused to sly pretense,
Does not reluct to state its sentiments;
I'm not at all embarrassed, and can proclaim
Wholeheartedly, without reserve or shame,
That she whom I most honor, hold most dear,
And whose devoted slave I am...
　　(*Gesturing toward Henriette*)
　　　　　is here.
Take no offense; you've nothing to resent:
You've made your choice, and so should be content.
Your charms enthralled me once, as many a sigh
And warm profession served to testify;

Mon coeur vous consacrait une flamme immortelle;
Mais vos yeux n'ont pas cru leur conquête assez belle.
J'ai souffert sous leur joug cent mépris différents:
Ils régnaient sur mon âme en superbes tyrans:
Et je me suis cherché, lassé de tant de peines,
Des vainqueurs plus humains et de moins rudes chaînes;
    (*Montrant Henriette*)
Je les ai rencontrés, madame, dans ces yeux,
Et de leurs traits[42] à jamais me seront précieux;
D'un regard pitoyable[43] ils ont séché mes larmes
Et n'ont pas dédaigné le rebut de vos charmes[44].
De si rares bontés m'ont si bien su toucher
Qu'il n'est rien qui ne puisse à mes fers arracher;
Et je n'ose maintenant vous conjurer, madame,
De ne vouloir tenter nul effort sur ma flamme,
De ne point essayer à[45] rappeler un coeur
Résolu de mourir dans cette douce ardeur.

ARMANDE

Hé! qui vous dit, monsieur, que l'on[46] ait cette envie,
Et que de vous enfin si fort on se soucie?
Je vous trouve plaisant[47] de vous le figurer,
Et bien impertinent de me le déclarer.

HENRIETTE

Hé! doucement, ma soeur. Où donc est la morale
Qui sait si bien régir la partie animale
Et retenir la bride aux efforts du courroux?

ARMANDE

Mais vous, qui m'en parlez, où la pratiquez-vous,
De répondre à l'amour que l'on vous fait paraître
Sans le congé[48] de ceux qui vous ont donné l'être?

I offered you a love which could not fade,
Yet you disdained the conquest you had made.
Beneath your tyrant gaze, my soul has borne
A hundred bitter slights, and every scorn,
Till, wearying at last of whip and chain,
It hungered for a bondage more humane.
Such have I found, *Madame*, in these fair eyes,
　　(*Gesturing once more toward Henriette*)
Whose kindness I shall ever love and prize:
They have not spurned the man you cast aside,
And, warmed by their regard, my tears have dried.
Now nothing could persuade me to be free
Of this most amiable captivity,
And I entreat you, Madam, do not strive
To cause my former feelings to revive,
Or sway my heart as once you did, for I
Propose to love this lady till I die.

ARMANDE

Well, Sir! What makes you fancy that one might
Regard you with a jealous appetite?
You're fatuous indeed to harbor such
A thought, and very brash to say as much.

HENRIETTE

Steady now, Sister. Where's that discipline
Of soul which reins one's lower nature in,
And keeps one's temper under firm command?

ARMANDE

And you, dear: are your passions well in hand
When you propose to wed a man without
The leave of those who brought your life about?

Sachez que le devoir vous soumet à leurs lois,
Qu'il ne vous est permis d'aimer que par leur choix,
Qu'ils ont sur votre coeur l'autorité suprême,
Et qu'il est criminel d'en disposer vous-même.

HENRIETTE

Je rends grâce aux bontés que vous me faites voir
De m'enseigner si bien les choses du devoir.
Mon coeur sur vos leçons veut régler sa conduite;
Et, pour vous faire voir, ma soeur, que j'en profite,
Clitandre, prenez soin d'appuyer votre amour
De l'agrément[49] de ceux dont j'ai reçu le jour;
Faites-vous sur mes voeux un pouvoir légitime
Et me donnez[50] moyen de vous aimer sans crime.

CLITANDRE

J'y vais de tous mes soins travailler hautement[51],
Et j'attendais de vous ce doux consentement.

ARMANDE

Vous triomphez, ma soeur, et faites une mine
A vous imaginer que cela me chagrine.

HENRIETTE

Moi, ma soeur? point du tout; Je sais que sur vos sens
Les droits de la raison sont toujours tout-puissants,
Et que, par les leçons qu'on prend dans la sagesse,
Vous êtes au-dessus d'une telle faiblesse.
Loin de vous soupçonner d'aucun chagrin[52], je croi
Qu'ici vous daignerez vous employer pour moi,
Appuyer sa demande et de votre suffrage
Presser l'heureux moment de notre mariage.
Je vous en sollicite; et, pour y travailler...

You owe your parents a complete submission,
And may not love except by their permission;
Your heart is theirs, and you may not bestow it;
To do so would be wicked, and you know it.

HENRIETTE

I'm very grateful to be thus instructed
In how these matters ought to be conducted.
And just to prove to you that I've imbibed
Your teachings, I shall do as you've prescribed:
Clitandre, I should thank you if you went
And gained from my dear parents their consent,
So that, without the risk of wickedness,
I could return the love which you profess.

CLITANDRE

Now that I have your gracious leave, I'll bend
My every effort towards that happy end.

ARMANDE

You look triumphant, Sister, and appear
To think me vexed by what has happened here.

HENRIETTE

By no means, Sister. I well know how you've checked
Your senses with the reins of intellect,
And how no foolish weakness could disturb
A heart so disciplined by wisdom's curb.
I'm far from thinking you upset; indeed,
I know you'll give me the support I need,
Help win my parents to Clitandre's side,
And speed the day when I may be his bride.
Do lend your influence, Sister, to promote—

ARMANDE

Votre petit esprit se mêle de railler,
Et d'un coeur qu'on vous jette on vous voit toute fière.

HENRIETTE

Tout jeté qu'est ce coeur, il ne vous déplaît guère;
Et si vos yeux sur moi le pouvaient ramasser,
Ils prendraient aisément le soin de se baisser.

ARMANDE

A répondre à cela je ne daigne descendre,
Et ce sont sots discours qu'il ne faut pas entendre.

HENRIETTE

C'est fort bien fait à vous, et vous nous faites voir
Des modérations qu'on ne peut concevoir.

ARMANDE

What childish teasing, Sister! And how you gloat
At having made a cast-off heart your prize!

HENRIETTE

Cast-off or not, it's one you don't despise.
Had you the chance to get it back from me,
You'd gladly pick it up on bended knee.

ARMANDE

I shall not stoop to answer that. I deem
This whole discussion silly in the extreme.

HENRIETTE

It is indeed, and you do well to end it.
Your self-control is great, and I commend it.

Scène III

CLITANDRE, HENRIETTE

———————

HENRIETTE

Votre sincère aveu ne l'a pas peu surprise.

CLITANDRE

Elle mérite assez une telle franchise,
Et toutes les hauteurs[53] de sa folle fierté
Sont dignes tout au moins de ma sincérité.
Mais puisqu'il m'est permis, je vais à votre père,
Madame...

HENRIETTE

　　Le plus sûr est de gagner ma mère:
Mon père est d'une humeur[54] à consentir à tout,
Mais il met peu de poids aux choses qu'il résout;
Il a reçu du ciel certaine bonté d'âme
Qui le soumet d'abord[55] à ce que veut sa femme;
C'est elle qui gouverne, et d'un ton absolu
Elle dicte pour loi ce qu'elle a résolu.
Je voudrais bien vous voir pour elle et pour ma tante
Une âme, je l'avoue, un peu plus complaisante,
Un esprit qui, flattant les visions[56] du leur,
Vous pût de leur estime attirer la chaleur.

Scene Three

CLITANDRE, HENRIETTE

HENRIETTE

Your frank avowal left her quite unnerved.

CLITANDRE

Such frankness was no less than she deserved;
Given her haughty airs and foolish pride,
My blunt words were entirely justified.
But now, since you have given me leave, I'll seek
Your father—

HENRIETTE

It's to Mother you should speak.
My gentle father would say yes, of course,
But his decrees, alas, have little force;
Heaven blessed him with a mild, concessive soul
Which yields in all things to his wife's control.
It's she who rules the house, requiring him
To treat as law her every royal whim.
I wish that you were more disposed to please
My mother, and indulge my Aunt Bélise,
By humoring their fancies, and thereby
Making them view you with a kindly eye.

CLITANDRE

Mon coeur n'a jamais pu, tant il est né sincère,
Même dans votre soeur flatter leur caractère,
Et les femmes docteurs[57] ne sont point de mon goût.
Je consens qu'une femme ait des clartés de tout,
Mais je ne lui veux point la passion choquante
De se rendre savante afin d'être savante;
Et j'aime que souvent, aux questions qu'on fait,
Elle sache ignorer les choses qu'elle sait;
De son étude enfin je veux qu'elle se cache[58],
Sans citer les auteurs, sans dire de grands mots
Et clouer de l'esprit à ses moindres propos.
Je respecte beaucoup madame votre mère,
Mais je ne puis du tout approuver se chimère
Et me rendre l'écho des choses qu'elle dit,
Aux encens[59] qu'elle donne à son héros d'esprit
Son monsieur Trissotin me chagrine, m'assomme,
Et j'enrage de voir qu'elle estime un tel homme,
Qu'elle nous mette au rang des grands et beaux esprits
Un benêt dont partout on siffle[60] les écrits,
Un pédant dont on voit la plume libérale[61]
D'officieux papiers fournir la halle[62].

HENRIETTE

Ses écrits, ses discours, tout m'en semble ennuyeux,
Et je me trouve assez votre goût et vos yeux[63];
Mais, comme sur ma mère il a une grande puissance,
Vous devez vous forcer à quelque complaisance.
Un amant fait sa cour où s'attache son coeur;
Il veut de tout le monde y gagner la faveur,
Et, pour n'avoir personne à sa flamme contraire[64],
Jusqu'au chien du logis il s'efforce de plaire.

CLITANDRE

My heart's too frank for that; I could not praise,
Even in your sister, such outlandish ways,
And female sages aren't my cup of tea.
A woman should know something, I agree,
Of every subject, but this proud desire
To pose as erudite I can't admire.
I like a woman who, though she may know
The answers, does not always let it show;
Who keeps her studies secret and, in fine,
Though she's enlightened, feels no need to shine
By means of pompous word and rare quotation
And brilliance on the slightest provocation.
I much respect your mother; nonetheless,
I can't encourage her in foolishness,
Agree with everything she says, and laud
Her intellectual hero—who's a fraud.
I loath her Monsieur Trissotin; how can
She so esteem so ludicrous a man,
And class with men of genius and of vision
A dunce whose works meet always with derision,
A bore whose dreadful books end, one and all,
As wrapping paper in some market stall?

HENRIETTE

All that he writes or speaks I find a bore;
I could agree with all you say, and more;
But since the creature has my mother's ear,
He's someone you should cultivate, I fear.
A lover seeks the good opinion of
All who surround the object of his love,
And, so that no one will oppose his passion,
Treats even the house-dog in a courtly fashion.

CLITANDRE

Oui, vous avez raison; mais monsieur Trissotin
M'inspire au fond de l'âme un dominant chagrin.
Je ne puis consentir, pour gagner ses suffrages,
A me déshonorer en prisant ses ouvrages,
C'est par eux qu'à mes yeux il a d'abord paru,
Et je le connaissais avant que[65] l'avoir vu.
Je vis, dans le fatras des écrits qu'il nous donne,
Ce qu'étale en tous lieux sa pédante personne,
La constante hauteur de sa présomption,
Cette intrépidité de bonne opinion,
Cet indolent état de confiance extrême
Qui le rend en tout temps si content de soi-même[66],
Qui fait qu'à son mérite incessamment il rit,
Qu'il se sait si bon gré de[67] tout ce qu'il écrit,
Et qu'il ne voudrait pas changer sa renommée
Contre tous les honneurs d'un général d'armée.

HENRIETTE

C'est d'avoir de bons yeux que de voir tout cela.

CLITANDRE

Jusques à sa figure encor[68] la chose alla,
Et je vis, par les vers qu'à la tête il nous jette,
De quel air il fallait que fût le poète;
Et j'en avais si bien deviné tous les traits
Que, rencontrant un homme un jour dans le Palais[69],
Je gageai que c'était Trissotin en personne,
Et je vis qu'en effet la gageure était bonne.

CLITANDRE

You're right; yet Trissotin, I must admit,
So irks me that there's no controlling it.
I can't, to gain his advocacy, stoop
To praise the works of such a nincompoop.
It was those works which introduced me to him;
Before I ever saw the man, I knew him;
From the vile way he wrote, I saw with ease
What, in the flesh, must be his qualities:
The absolute presumption, the complete
And dauntless nature of his self-conceit,
The calm assurance of superior worth
Which renders him the smuggest man on earth,
So that he stands in awe and hugs himself
Before his volumes ranged upon the shelf,
And would not trade his baseless reputation
For that of any general in the nation.

HENRIETTE

If you could see all that, you've got good eyes.

CLITANDRE

I saw still more; for I could visualize,
By studying his dreadful poetry,
Just what the poet's lineaments must be;
I pictured his so truly that, one day,
Seeing a foppish man in the Palais,
I said, "That's Trissotin, by God!"—and found,
Upon enquiry, that my hunch was sound.

LES FEMMES SAVANTES

HENRIETTE

Quel conte!

CLITANDRE

Non: je dis la chose comme elle est.
Mais je vois votre tante. Agréez, s'il vous plaît,
Que mon coeur lui déclare ici notre mystère[70]
Et gagne sa faveur auprès de votre mère.

HENRIETTE

What a wild story!

CLITANDRE

Not at all; it's true.
But here's your aunt. If you'll permit me to,
I'll tell her of our hopes, in hopes that she
Will urge your mother to approve of me.

Scène IV

CLITANDRE, BÉLISE

CLITANDRE

Souffrez, pour vous parler, madame, qu'un amant
Prenne l'occasion de cet heureux moment
Et se découvre à vous de[71] la sincère flamme...

BÉLISE

Ah! tout beau![72] Gardez-vous de m'ouvrir trop votre âme.
Si je vous ai su mettre au rang de mes amants,
Contentez-vous des yeux pour vos seuls truchements,
Et ne m'expliquez point par un autre langage
Des désirs qui chez moi[73], passent pour un outrage.
Aimez-moi, soupirez, brûlez pour mes appas;
Mais qu'il me soit permis de ne le savoir pas.
Je puis fermer les yeux sur vos flammes[74] secrètes,
Tant que vous tiendrez aux muets interprètes[75];
Mais, si la bouche vient à s'en vouloir mêler,
Pour jamais de ma vue il vous faut exiler.

CLITANDRE

Des projets de mon coeur ne prenez point d'alarme.
Henriette, madame, est l'objet qui me charme,
Et je viens ardemment conjurer vos bontés
De seconder l'amour que j'ai pour ses beautés.

Scene Four

CLITANDRE, BÉLISE

CLITANDRE

Madam, permit a lover's heart to seize
This happy opportunity, if you please,
To tell you of his passion, and reveal—

BÉLISE

Hold, Sir! Don't say too baldly what you feel.
If you belong, sir, to the ranks of those
Who love me, let your eyes alone disclose
Your sentiments, and do not tell me bluntly
Of coarse desires which only could affront me.
Adore me if you will, but do not show it
In such a way that I'll be forced to know it;
Worship me inwardly, and I shall brook it
If, through your silence, I can overlook it;
But should you dare to speak of it outright,
I'll banish you forever from my sight.

CLITANDRE

My passions, Madam, need cause you no alarms;
It's Henriette who's won me by her charms,
And I entreat your generous soul to aid me
In my design to wed that charming lady.

BÉLISE

Ah! certes, le détour est d'esprit[76], je l'avoue.
Ce subtil faux-fuyant[77] mérite qu'on le loue;
Et, dans tous les romans où j'ai jeté les yeux,
Je n'ai rien rencontré de plus ingénieux.

CLITANDRE

Ceci n'est point du tout un trait d'esprit, madame,
Et c'est un pur aveu de ce que j'ai dans l'âme.
Les cieux, par les liens d'une immuable ardeur,
Aux beautés d'Henriette ont attaché mon coeur;
Henriette me tient sous son aimable empire[78],
Et l'hymen d'Henriette[79] est le bien où j'aspire.
Vous y pouvez beaucoup, et tout ce que je veux,
C'est que vous y daigniez favoriser mes voeux.

BÉLISE

Je vois où doucement veut aller la demande,
Et je sais sous ce nom ce qu'il faut que j'entende[80].
La figure[81] est adroite et, pour n'en point sortir,
Aux choses que mon coeur m'offre à vous repartir,
Je dirai qu'Henriette à l'hymen est rebelle,
Et que sans rien prétendre[82] il faut brûler pour elle.

CLITANDRE

Eh! madame, à quoi bon un pareil embarras[83]?
Et pourquoi voulez-vous penser ce qui n'est pas?

BÉLISE

Mon Dieu, point de façons[84]: cessez de vous défendre
De ce que vos regards m'ont souvent fait entendre.

BÉLISE

Ah, what a subtle dodge; you should be proud;
You're very artful, it must be allowed;
In all the novels that I've read, I've never
Encountered any subterfuge so clever.

CLITANDRE

Madam, I meant no witty indirection;
I've spoken truly of my heart's affection.
By Heaven's will, by ties that cannot part,
I'm bound to Henriette with all my heart;
It's Henriette I cherish, as I've said,
And Henriette whom I aspire to wed.
All that I ask of you is that you lend
Your influence to help me gain that end.

BÉLISE

I well devine the hopes which you have stated,
And how the name you've used should be translated.
A clever substitution, Sir; and I
Shall use the selfsame code in my reply:
"Henriette" disdains to wed, and those who burn
For her must hope for nothing in return.

CLITANDRE

Madam, why make things difficult? Why insist
Upon supposing what does not exist?

BÉLISE

Good heavens, Sir, don't stand on ceremony,
Denying what your looks have often shown me.

Il suffit que l'on est[85] contente du détour
Dont s'est adroitement avisé votre amour,
Et que, sous la figure[86] où le respect l'engage,
On veut bien se résoudre à souffrir son hommage,
Pourvu que ses transports[87] par l'honneur éclairés,
N'offrent à mes autels[88] que des voeux épurés.

CLITANDRE

Mais...

BÉLISE

Adieu. Pour ce coup, ceci doit vous suffire,
Et je vous ai plus dit que je ne voulais dire.

CLITANDRE

Mais votre erreur...

BÉLISE

Laissez. Je rougis maintenant,
Et ma pudeur s'est fait un effort surprenant.

CLITANDRE

Je veux être pendu si je vous aime, et sage...

BÉLISE

Non, non, je ne veux rien entendre davantage.
                    (Elle sort)

Let it suffice, Sir, that I am contented
With this oblique approach you have invented,
And that, beneath such decorous disguise,
Your homage is acceptable in my eyes,
Provided that you make no overture
Which is not noble, rarefied, and pure.

CLITANDRE

But—

BÉLISE

Hush. Farewell. It's time our talk was ended.
I've said, already, more than I intended.

CLITANDRE

You're quite mistaken—

BÉLISE

I'm blushing, can't you see?
All this has overtaxed my modesty.

CLITANDRE

I'm hanged if I love you Madam! This is absurd.

BÉLISE

No, no, I mustn't hear another word.
                    (*She exits*)

CLITANDRE

Diantre[89] soit la folle avec ses visions!
A-t-on rien vu d'égal à ses préventions[90]?
Allons commettre un autre au soin[91] que l'on me don
Et prenons le secours d'une sage personne.

CLITANDRE

The devil take her and her addled brain!
What stubborn fancies she can entertain!
Well, I'll turn elsewhere, and shall hope to find
Support from someone with a balanced mind.

Act II

Scène Première

ARISTE

ARISTE

Oui, je vous porterai la réponse au plus tôt.
J'appuierai, presserai, ferai tout ce qu'il faut.
Qu'un amant, pour un mot, a de choses à dire,
Et qu'impatiemment il veut ce qu'il désire!
Jamais...

Scene One

ARISTE

ARISTE

Yes, yes, I'll urge and plead as best I can, Sir,
Then hasten back to you and bring his answer.
Lover! How very much they have to say,
And what extreme impatience they display!
Never—

Scène II

CHRYSALE, ARISTE

ARISTE

Ah! Dieu vous gard'[92], mon frère.

CHYSALE

Et vous aussi, mon frère.

ARISTE

Savez-vous ce qui m'amène ici?

CHRYSALE

Non; mais si vous voulez, je suis prêt à l'apprendre.

ARISTE

Depuis assez longtemps vous connaissez Clitandre?

CHRYSALE

Sans doute, et je le vois qui fréquente chez nous.

ARISTE

En quelle estime[93] est-il, mon frère, auprès de vous?

Scene Two

CHRYSALE, ARISTE

ARISTE

Ah! God be with you, Brother dear.

CHRYSALE

And you, dear Brother.

ARISTE

D'you know what brings me here?

CHRYSALE

No, but I'll gladly learn of it; do tell.

ARISTE

I think you know Clitandre rather well?

CHRYSALE

Indeed; he calls here almost every day.

ARISTE

And what is your opinion of him, pray?

CHRYSALE

D'homme d'honneur, d'esprit, de coeur, et de conduite[94];
Et je vois peu de gens qui soient de son mérite.

ARISTE

Certain désir qu'il a conduit ici mes pas,
Et je me réjouis que vous en fassiez cas.

CHRYSALE

Je connus feu son père en mon voyage à Rome.

ARISTE

Fort bien.

CHRYSALE

C'était, mon frère, un fort bon gentilhomme.

ARISTE

On le dit.

CHRYSALE

Nous n'avions alors que vingt-huit ans,
Et nous étions, ma foi, tout deux de verts galants[95].

ARISTE

Je le crois.

CHRYSALE

He's a man of honor, breeding, wit, and spirit;
I know few lads of comparable merit.

ARISTE

Well, I am here at his request; I'm glad
to learn that you think highly of the lad.

CHRYSALE

I knew his father well, during my stay
In Rome.

ARISTE

Ah, good.

CHRYSALE

A fine man.

ARISTE

So they say.

CHRYSALE

We were both young then, twenty-eight or so,
And a pair of dashing gallants, I'll have you know.

ARISTE

I'm sure of it.

CHRYSALE

Nous donnions chez[96] les dames romaines.
Et tout le monde là parlait de nos fredaines;
Nous faisions des jaloux.

ARISTE

Voilà qui va des mieux
Mais venons au sujet qui m'amène en ces lieux.

CHRYSALE

Oh, those dark-eyed Roman maids!
The whole town talked about our escapades,
And weren't the husbands jealous!

ARISTE

Ho! No doubt!
But let me broach the matter I came about.

Scène III

BÉLISE, CHRYSALE, ARISTE

ARISTE

Clitandre auprès de vous me fait son interprète,
Et son coeur est épris des grâces d'Henriette

CHRYSALE

Quoi! de ma fille?

ARISTE

Oui; Clitandre en est charmé[97],
Et je ne vis jamais amant plus enflammé.

BÉLISE

Non, non je vous entends. Vous ignorez l'histoire,
Et l'affaire n'est pas ce que vous pouvez croire.

ARISTE

Comment, ma soeur?

BÉLISE

Clitandre abuse vos esprits[98],
Et c'est d'autre objet que son coeur est épris.

ARISTE

Vous raillez. Ce n'est pas Henriette qu'il aime?

Scene Three

BÉLISE, CHRYSALE, ARISTE

———————

ARISTE

I'm here to speak for young Clitandre, and let
You know of his deep love for Henriette.

CHRYSALE

He loves my daughter?

ARISTE

    Yes. Upon my honor,
I've never seen such passion; he dotes upon her.

BÉLISE

No, no; I see what's happened. You're unaware
Of the true character of this affair.

ARISTE

What, Sister?

BÉLISE

    Clitandre has misled you, Brother:
The passion which he feels is for another.

ARISTE

Oh, come. He doesn't love Henriette? Then how—

BÉLISE

BÉLISE

Non, j'en suis assurée.

ARISTE

Il ma l'a dit lui-même.

BÉLISE

Eh! oui.

ARISTE

Vous me voyez, ma soeur, chargé par lui
D'en faire la demande à son père aujourd'hui.

BÉLISE

Fort bien.

ARISTE

Et son amour même m'a fait instance
De presser les moments d'une telle alliance.

BÉLISE

Encore mieux. On ne peut tromper plus galamment.
Henriette, entre nous, est un amusement,
Un voile ingénieux, un prétexte, mon frère,
A couvrir d'autres feux dont je sais le mystère,
Et je veux bien tous deux vous mettre hors d'erreur.

I'm certain of it.

ARISTE

He said he did, just now.

BÉLISE

Of course.

ARISTE

He sent me here, please understand,
To ask her father for the lady's hand.

BÉLISE

Splendid.

ARISTE

What's more, his ardor is so great
That I'm to urge an early wedding date.

BÉLISE

Oh, how delightful; what obliquity!
We use the name of "Henriette," you see,
As a code word and camouflage concealing
The actual object of his tender feeling.
But I'll consent, now, to enlighten you.

ARISTE

Mais puisque vous savez tant de choses, ma soeur,
Dites-nous, s'il vous plaît, cet autre objet qu'il aime.

BÉLISE

Vous le voulez savoir?

ARISTE

Oui. Quoi?

BÉLISE

Moi.

ARISTE

Vous?

BÉLISE

Moi-même.

ARISTE

Hai[99], ma soeur!

BÉLISE

Qu'est-ce donc que veut dire ce hai?
Et qu'a de surprenant le discours que je fais?
On est faite d'un air[100], je pense, à pouvoir dire
Qu'on n'a pas pour un coeur[101] soumis à son empire;
Et Dorante, Damis, Cléonte et Lycidas
Peuvent bien faire voir qu'on a quelques appas.

ARISTE

Well, Sister, since you know so much, please do
Tell us with whom his true affections lie.

BÉLISE

You wish to know?

ARISTE

I do.

BÉLISE

It's I.

ARISTE

You?

BÉLISE

I.

ARISTE

Well, Sister!

BÉLISE

What do you mean by *well*? My word,
Why should you look so surprised at what you've heard?
My charms are evident, in my frank opinion,
And more than one heart's under their dominion.
Dorante, Damis, Cléonte, Valère—all these
Are proof of my attractive qualities.

ARISTE

Ces gens vous aiment?

BÉLISE

Oui, de toute leur puissance.

ARISTE

Ils vous l'ont dit?

BÉLISE

Aucun n'a pris cette licence[102]:
Ils m'ont su révérer si fort jusqu'à ce jour
Qu'il ne m'ont jamais dit un mot de leur amour.
Mais, pour m'offrir leur coeur et vouer leur service,
Les muets truchements ont tous fait leur office.

ARISTE

On ne voit presque point céans[103] venir Damis.

BÉLISE

C'est pour me faire voir un respect plus soumis.

ARISTE

De mots piquants[104] partout Dorante vous outrage.

BÉLISE

Ce sont emportements d'une jalouse rage.

Act II Scene Three

ARISTE

These men all love you?

BÉLISE

Yes, with all their might.

ARISTE

They've said so?

BÉLISE

None has been so impolite:
They've worshipped me as one from Heaven above,
And not presumed to breathe a word of love.
Mute signs, however, have managed to impart
The keen devotion of each humble heart.

ARISTE

Damis is almost never seen here. Why?

BÉLISE

His reverence for me has made him shy.

ARISTE

Dorante reviles you in the harshest fashion.

BÉLISE

He's seized, at times, by fits of jealous passion.

ARISTE

Cléonte et Lycidas ont pris femme tous deux.

BÉLISE

C'est par désespoir où j'ai réduit leurs feux.

ARISTE

Ma foi, ma chère soeur, vision toute claire[105].

CHRYSALE

De ces chimères-là vous devez vous défaire.

BÉLISE

Ah! chimères? Ce sont des chimères, dit-on?
Chimères, moi? Vraiment, chimères est fort bon!
Je me réjouis fort de chimères, mes frères,
Et je ne savais pas que j'eusse des chimères.

ARISTE

Cléonte has lately married; so has Valère.

BÉLISE

That was because I drove them to despair.

ARISTE

Sister, you're prone to fantasies, I fear.

CHRYSALE (*to Bélise*)

Get rid of these chimeras, Sister dear.

BÉLISE

Chimeras! Well! Chimeras, did you say?
I have chimeras! Well, how very gay!
May all your thoughts, dear Brothers, be as clear as
Those which you dared, just now, to call *chimeras!*

Scène IV

CHRYSALE, ARISTE

———————————

CHRYSALE

Notre soeur est folle, oui[106].

ARISTE

Cela croît tous les jours.
Mais encore une fois, reprenons le discours[107].
Clitandre vous demande Henriette pour femme:
Voyez quelle réponse on doit faire à sa flamme.

CHRYSALE

Faut-il le demander? J'y consens de bon coeur,
Et tiens son alliance à singulier honneur.

ARISTE

Vous savez que de bien il n'a pas l'abondance,
Que...

CHRYSALE

C'est un interêt[108] qui n'est pas d'importance:
Il est riche en vertu, cela vaut des trésors;
Et puis son père et moi n'étions qu'un en deux corps.

Scene Four

CHRYSALE, ARISTE

———————

CHRYSALE

Our sister's mad.

ARISTE

  And growing madder daily.
But, once more, let's discuss our business, may we?
Clitandre longs to marry Henriette,
And asks your blessing. What answer shall he get?

CHRYSALE

No need to ask. I readily agree.
His wish does honor to my family.

ARISTE

He has, as you well know, no great amount
Of worldly goods—

CHRYSALE

      Ah, gold's of no account:
He's rich in virtue, that most precious ore;
His father and I were bosom friends, what's more.

ARISTE

Parlons à votre femme, et voyons à la rendre
Favorable...

CHRYSALE

Il suffit, je l'accepte pour gendre.

ARISTE

Oui; mais, pour appuyer votre consentement,
Mon frère, il n'est pas mal d'avoir son agrément.
Allons...

CHRYSALE

Vous moquez-vous? Il n'est pas nécessaire.
Je réponds de la femme, et prends sur moi l'affaire.

ARISTE

Mais...

CHRYSALE

Laissez faire, dis-je, et n'appréhendez pas.
Je la vais disposer aux choses de ce pas[109].

ARISTE

Soit. Je vais là-dessus sonder votre Henriette,
Et reviendrai savoir...

CHRYSALE

C'est une affaire faite.
Et je vais à ma femme en parler sans délai.

ARISTE

Let's go make certain that your wife concurs.

CHRYSALE

I've given my consent; no need for hers.

ARISTE

True, Brother; still, 'twould do no harm if your
Decision had her strong support, I'm sure.
Let's both go—

CHRYSALE

Nonsense, that's a needless move;
I'll answer for my wife. She will approve.

ARISTE

But—

CHRYSALE

No. Enough. I'll deal with her. Don't worry.
The business will be settled in a hurry.

ARISTE

So be it. I'll go consult with Henriette,
And then—

CHRYSALE

The thing's as good as done; don't fret.
I'll tell my wife about it, without delay.

Scène V

———————

MARTINE

Me voilà bien chanceuse[110]! hélas! l'on dit bien vrai:
Qui veut noyer son chien l'accuse de la rage[111],
Et service d'autrui n'est pas un héritage.

CHRYSALE

Qu'est-ce donc? Qu'avez-vous, Martine?

MARTINE

    Ce que j'ai?

CHRYSALE

Oui.

MARTINE

    J'ai que l'on me donne aujourd'hui mon congé,
Monsieur.

CHRYSALE

    Votre congé?

Scene Five

MARTINE, CHRYSALE

MARTINE

Ain't that my luck! It's right, what people say—
When you hang a dog, first give him a bad name.
Domestic service! It's a losing game.

CHRYSALE

Well, well, Martine! What's up?

MARTINE

You want to know?

CHRYSALE

Why, yes.

MARTINE

What's up is, Madam's let me go.

CHRYSALE

She's let you go?

MARTINE

Oui. Madame me chasse.

CHRYSALE

Je n'entends pas cela. Comment?

MARTINE

On me menace,
Si je ne sors d'ici, de me bailler[112] cent coups.

CHRYSALE

Non, vous demeurerez; je suis content de vous.
Ma femme bien souvent a la tête un peu chaude:
Et je ne veux pas, moi...

MARTINE

Yes, given me the sack.

CHRYSALE

But why? Whatever for?

MARTINE

She says she'll whack
Me black and blue if I don't clear out of here.

CHRYSALE

No, you shall stay; you've served me well, my dear.
My wife's a bit short-tempered at times, and fussy:
But this won't do. I'll—

Scène VI

PHILAMINTE, BELISE, CHRYSALE, MARTINE

PHILAMINTE

Quoi! je vous vois, maraude[113]!
Vite, sortez, friponne; allons, quittez ces lieux,
Et ne vous présentez jamais devant mes yeux.

CHRYSALE

Tout doux[114]!

PHILAMINTE

Non, c'en est fait.

CHRYSALE

Eh!

PHILAMINTE

Je veux qu'elle sorte.

CHRYSALE

Mais, qu'a-t-elle commis, pour vouloir de la sorte...

PHILAMINTE

Quoi! vous la soutenez?

Scene Six

PHILAMINTE, BÉLISE, CHRYSALE, MARTINE

PHILAMINTE (*seeing Martine*)

What! Still here, you hussy!
Be off, you trollop; leave my house this minute,
And mind you never again set foot within it!

CHRYSALE

Gently, now.

PHILAMINTE

No, it's settled.

CHRYSALE

But—

PHILAMINTE

Off with her!

CHRYSALE

What crime has she committed, to incur—

PHILAMINTE

So! You defend the girl!

CHRYSALE

En aucune façon.

PHILAMINTE

Prenez-vous son parti contre moi?

CHRYSALE

Mon Dieu, non,
Je ne fais seulement que demander son crime.

PHILAMINTE

Suis-je pour[115] la chasser sans cause légitime?

CHRYSALE

Je ne dis pas cela; mais il faut de nos gens...

PHILAMINTE

Non, elle sortira, vous dis-je, de céans.

CHRYSALE

Hé bien, oui. Vous dit-on quelque chose là-contre?

PHILAMINTE

Je ne veux point d'obstacle aux désirs que je montre.

CHRYSALE

D'accord.

CHRYSALE

No, that's not so.

PHILAMINTE

Are you taking her side against me?

CHRYSALE

Heavens, no;
I merely asked the nature of her offense.

PHILAMINTE

Would I, without good reason, send her hence?

CHRYSALE

Of course not; but employers should be just—

PHILAMINTE

Enough! I bade her leave, and leave she must.

CHRYSALE

Quite so, quite so. Has anyone denied it?

PHILAMINTE

I won't be contradicted. I can't abide it.

CHRYSALE

Agreed.

PHILAMINTE

Et vous devez, en raisonnable époux,
Etre pour moi contre elle et prendre mon courroux.

CHRYSALE

Aussi fais-je[116]. Oui, ma femme avec raison vous chasse,
Coquine[117], et votre crime est indigne de grâce.

MARTINE

Qu'est-ce donc que j'ai fait?

CHRYSALE (*bas*)

Ma foi, je ne sais pas.

PHILAMINTE

Elle est d'humeur encore à n'en faire aucun cas.

CHRYSALE

A-t-elle, pour donner matière à votre haine,
Cassé quelque miroir ou quelque porcelaine?

PHILAMINTE

Voudrais-je la chasser, et vous figurez-vous
Que pour si peu de chose on se met en courroux?

CHRYSALE (*A Martine*)

Qu'est-ce à dire?
(*A Philaminte*) L'affaire est donc considérable?

PHILAMINTE

If you were a proper husband, you
Would take my side, and share my outrage, too.

CHRYSALE

I do, dear.
                (*Turning towards Martine*)
        Wench! My wife is right to rid
This house of one who's done the thing you did.

MARTINE

What did I do?

CHRYSALE (*aside*)

Alas, you have me there.

PHILAMINTE

She takes a light view, still, of this affair.

CHRYSALE

What caused your anger? How did all this begin?
Did she break some mirror, or piece of porcelain?

PHILAMINTE

Do you suppose that I'd be angry at her,
And bid her leave, for such a trifling matter?

CHRYSALE (*to Martine*)

        What can this mean?
(*To Philaminte*) Is the crime, then, very great?

PHILAMINTE

Sans doute. Me voit-on[118] femme déraisonnable?

CHRYSALE

Est-ce qu'elle a laissé, d'un esprit négligent,
Dérober quelque aiguière[119] ou quelque plat d'argent?

PHILAMINTE

Cela ne serait rien.

CHRYSALE

Oh! oh! Peste la belle!
Quoi! l'avez-vous surprise à n'être pas fidèle[120]?

PHILAMINTE

C'est pis que tout cela.

CHRYSALE

Pis que tout cela?

PHILAMINTE

Pis.

CHRYSALE

Comment, diantre, friponne! Euh! a-t-elle commis...

PHILAMINTE

Of course it is. Would I exaggerate?

CHRYSALE

Did she, perhaps, by inadvertence, let
Some vase be stolen, or some china set?

PHILAMINTE

That would be nothing.

CHRYSALE (*to Martine*)

Blast, girl, what can this be?
(*to Philaminte*)
Have you caught the chit in some dishonesty?

PHILAMINTE

Far worse than that.

CHRYSALE

Far worse than that?

PHILAMINTE

Far worse.

CHRYSALE (*to Martine*)

For shame, you strumpet! (*To Philaminte*) Has she been so
perverse—

PHILAMINTE

Elle a, d'une insolence à nulle autre pareille,
Après trente leçons, insulté[121] mon oreille
Par l'impropriété d'un mot sauvage et bas
Qu'en termes décisifs condamne Vaugelas[122].

CHRYSALE

Est-ce là...

PHILAMINTE

Quoi! toujours, malgré nos remontrances,
Heurter le fondement de toutes les sciences,
La grammaire, qui sait régenter jusqu'aux rois
Et les fait la main haute obéir à ses lois[123]!

CHRYSALE

Du plus grand des forfaits je la croyais coupable.

PHILAMINTE

Quoi! vous ne trouvez pas ce crime impardonnable?

CHRYSALE

Si fait.

PHILAMINTE

Je voudrais bien que vous l'excusassiez!

CHRYSALE

Je n'ai garde[124]!

PHILAMINTE

This creature, who for insolence has no peer,
Has, after thirty lessons, shocked my ear
by uttering a low, plebeian word
Which Vaugelas deems unworthy to be heard.

CHRYSALE

Is *that*—?

PHILAMINTE

And she persists in her defiance
Of that which is the basis of all science—
Grammar! Which even the mightiest must obey,
And whose pure laws hold princes in their sway.

CHRYSALE

I was sure she'd done the worst thing under the sun.

PHILAMINTE

What! You don't find it monstrous, what she's done?

CHRYSALE

Oh, yes.

PHILAMINTE

I'd love to hear you plead her case!

CHRYSALE

Not I!

BÉLISE

Il est vrai que ce sont des pitiés:
Toute construction est par elle détruite,
Et des lois du langage on l'a cent fois instruite.

MARTINE

Tout ce que vous prêchez est, je crois, bel et bon;
Mais je ne saurais, moi, parler votre jargon.

PHILAMINTE

L'imprudente! Appeler un jargon le langage
Fondé sur la raison et sur le bel usage[125]!

MARTINE

Quand on se fait entendre, on parle toujours bien,
Et tout vos biaux dictons[126] ne servent pas de rien.

PHILAMINTE

Hé bien, ne voilà pas encore de son style!
"Ne servent pas de rien!"

BÉLISE

O cervelle indocile!
Faut-il qu'avec les soins qu'on prend incessamment
On ne te puisse apprendre à parler congrûment[127]!
De *pas* mis avec *rien* tu fais la récidive,
Et c'est, comme on t'a dit, trop d'une négative.

MARTINE

Mon Dieu! je n'avons pas étugué[128] comme vous,
Et je parlons tout droit comme on parle cheux[129] nous.

BÉLISE

It's true, her speech is a disgrace.
How long we've taught her language and its laws!
Yet still she butchers every phrase or clause.

MARTINE

I'm sure your preachings is all well and good,
But I wouldn't talk your jargon if I could.

PHILAMINTE

She dares describes as jargon a speech that's based
On reason, and good usage, and good taste!

MARTINE

If people get the point, that's speech to me;
Fine words don't have no use that I can see.

PHILAMINTE

Hark! There's a sample of her style again!
"Don't have no!"

BÉLISE

O ineducable brain!
How futile have our efforts been to teach
Your stubborn mind the rules of proper speech!
You've coupled *don't* with *no*. I can't forgive
That pleonasm, that double negative.

MARTINE

Good Lord, Ma'am, I ain't studious like you;
I just talk plain, the way my people do.

PHILAMINTE

Ah! peut-on y tenir?

BÉLISE

Quel solécisme horrible!

PHILAMINTE

En voilà pour tuer une oreille sensible!

BÉLISE

Ton esprit, je l'avoue, est bien matériel.
Je n'est qu'un singulier, *avons* est pluriel.
Veux-tu toute ta vie offenser la grammaire?

MARTINE

Qui parle d'offenser grand'mère[130] ni grand-père?

PHILAMINTE

Oh ciel!

BÉLISE

Grammaire est prise à contresens par toi,
Et je t'ai déjà dit d'où vient ce mot.

MARTINE

Ma foi,
Qu'il vienne de Chaillot, d'Auteuil ou de Pontoise
Cela ne me fait rien.

PHILAMINTE

What ghastly slecisms!

BÉLISE

I could faint!

PHILAMINTE

How the ear shudders at the sound of "ain't"!

BÉLISE (*to Martine*)

With ignorance like yours, one struggles vainly.
"Plain" is an adjective; the adverb's "plainly."
Shall grammar be abused by you forever?

MARTINE

Me abuse Gramma? Or Grampa either? Never!

PHILAMINTE

Dear God!

BÉLISE

What I said was "grammar." You misheard.
I've told you about the origin of the word.

MARTINE

Let it come from Passy, Pontoise, or Chaillot;
It's Greek to me.

BELISE

Quelle âme villageoise!
La grammaire, du verbe et du nominatif,
Comme de l'adjectif avec le substantif,
Nous enseigne les lois.

MARTINE

J'ai, madame, à vous dire
Que je ne connais point ces gens-là.

PHILAMINTE

Quel martyre.

BELISE

Ce sont les noms des mots, et l'on doit regarder
En quoi c'est qu'il les faut faire ensemble accorder.

MARTINE

Qu'ils s'accordent entre eux, ou se gourment[132], qu'importe?

PHILAMINTE (*à sa belle-soeur*)

Eh! mon Dieu, finissez un discours de la sorte.
  (*A son mari*)
Vous ne voulez pas, vous, ma la faire sortir?

CHRYSALE

(*A part*) Si fait. A son caprice, il ne faut consentir.
                    (*A Martine*)
Va, ne l'irrite point; retire-toi, Martine.

BÉLISE

Alas, what *do* you know,
You peasant? It is grammar which lays down
The laws which govern adjective and noun,
And verb, and subject.

MARTINE

Madam, I'd just be lying
If I said I knew those people.

PHILAMINTE

Oh, how trying!

BÉLISE

Girl, those are parts of speech, and we must be
At pains to make those parts of speech agree.

MARTINE

Let them agree or squabble, what does it matter?

PHILAMINTE (*to her sister-in-law*)

Ah, mercy, let's be done with all this chatter!
    (*to her husband*)
Sir! Will you bid her go and leave me in peace?

CHRYSALE

Yes, yes. (*Aside*) I must give in to her caprice.
                (*to Martine*)
Martine, don't vex her further; you'd best depart.

PHILAMINTE

Comment! vous avez peur d'offenser la coquine?
Vous lui parlez d'un ton tout à fait obligeant!

CHRYSALE

(Haut) Moi? point; Allons sortez.
        (Bas, A Martine)
               Va-t'en, ma pauvre enfant.

PHILAMINTE

So, you're afraid to wound her little heart!
The hussy! Must you be so sweet and mild?

CHRYSALE

Of course not. (*Loudly*) Wench, be off!
        (*Softly, to Martine*)
                        Go, go, poor child.

Scène VII

PHILAMINTE, CHRYSALE, BÉLISE

───────────────

CHRYSALE

Vous êtes satisfaite, et la voilà partie;
Mais je n'approuve point une telle sortie[133]:
C'est une fille propre aux choses qu'elle fait,
Et vous me la chassez pour un maigre sujet.

PHILAMINTE

Vous voulez que toujours je l'aie à mon service,
Pour mettre incessamment mon oreille au supplice,
Pour rompre toute loi d'usage et de raison
Par un barbare amas de vices d'oraison[134],
De mots estropiés, cousus par intervalles,
De proverbes traînés dans les ruisseaux des halles[135]?

BÉLISE

Il est vrai que l'on sue à souffrir ses discours.
Elle y met Vaugelas en pièces tous les jours;
Et les moindres défauts de ce grossier génie[136]
Sont ou le pléonasme ou la cacophonie[137].

CHRYSALE

Qu'importe qu'elle manque aux lois de Vaugelas,
Pourvu qu'à la cuisine elle ne manque pas?
J'aime bien mieux, pour moi, qu'en épluchant ses herbes
Elle accommode mal les noms avec les verbes,

Scene Seven

CHRYSALE

Well, you have had your way, and she is gone;
But I don't think much of the way you've carried on.
The girl is good at what she does, and you've
Dismissed her for a trifle. I don't approve.

PHILAMINTE

Would you have me keep her in my service here
To give incessant anguish to my ear
By constant barbarisms, and the breach
Of every law of reason and good speach,
Patching the mangled discourse which she utters
With coarse expressions from the city's gutters?

BÉLISE

It's true, her talk can drive one out of one's wits.
Each day, she tears dear Vaugelas to bits,
And the least failings of this pet of yours
Are vile cacophonies and non sequiturs.

CHRYSALE

Who care if she offends some grammar book,
So long as she doesn't offend us as a cook?
If she makes a tasty salad, it seems to me
Her subjects and her verbs need not agree.

Et redise cent fois un bas ou méchant[138] mot
Que de brûler ma viande ou saler trop mon pot.
Je vis de bonne soupe et non de beau langage.
Vaugelas n'apprend point à bien faire un potage;
Et Malherbe et Balzac[139], si savant en beaux mots,
En cuisine, peut-être, auraient été des sots.

PHILAMINTE

Que ce discours grossier terriblement assomme!
Et quelle indignité, pour ce qui s'appelle homme[140],
D'être baissé sans cesse aux soins matériels,
Au lieu de se hausser vers les spirituels!
Le corps, cette guenille, est-il d'une importance,
D'un prix à mériter seulement qu'on y pense?
Et ne devons-nous pas laisser cela bien loin?

CHRYSALE

Oui, mon corps est moi-même, et j'en veux prendre soin.
Guenille, si l'on veut, ma guenille m'est chère.

BÉLISE

Le corps avec l'esprit fait figure[141], mon frère;
Mais, si vous en croyez tout le monde savant,
L'esprit doit sur le corps prendre le pas devant,
Et notre plus grand soin, notre première instance[142],
Doit être à le nourrir du suc de la science.

CHRYSALE

Ma foi, si vous songez à nourrir votre esprit,
C'est de viande bien creuse[143], à ce que chacun dit;
Et vous n'avez nul soin, nulle solicitude,
Pour...

Let all her talk be barbarous, if she'll not
Burn up my beef or oversalt the pot.
It's food, not language, that I'm nourished by.
Vaugelas can't teach you how to bake a pie;
Malherbe, Balzac, for all their learnèd rules,
Might, in a kitchen, have been utter fools.

PHILAMINTE

I'm stunned by what you've said, and shocked at seeing
How you, who claim the rank of human being,
Rather than rise on spiritual wings,
Give all your care to base, material things.
This rag, the body—does it matter so?
Should its desire detain us here below?
Should we not soar aloft, and scorn to heed it?

CHRYSALE

My body is myself, and I aim to feed it.
It's a rag, perhaps, but one of which I'm fond.

BÉLISE

Brother, 'twixt flesh and spirit there's a bond;
Yet, as the best minds of the age have stated,
The claims of flesh must be subordinated,
And it must be our chief delight and care
To feast the soul on philosophic fare.

CHRYSALE

I don't know what your soul's been eating of late,
But it's not a balanced diet, at any rate;
You show no womanly solicitude
For—

111

PHILAMINTE

Ah! *sollicitude* à mon oreille est rude;
Il pue étrangement son ancienneté.

BÉLISE

Il est vrai que le mot est bien collet monté[144].

CHRYSALE

Voulez-vous que je dise? Il faut qu'enfin j'éclate,
Que je lève le masque et décharge ma rate[145].
De folles on vous traite, et j'ai fort sur le coeur...

PHILAMINTE

Comment donc?

CHRYSALE

C'est à vous que je parle, ma soeur.
Le moindre solécisme en parlant[146] vous irrite;
Mais vous en faites, vous, d'étranges en conduite.
Vos livres éternels ne me contentent pas;
Et, hors un gros Plutarque[147] à mettre mes rabats,
Vous devriez brûler tout ce meuble inutile[148]
Et laisser la science aux docteurs de la ville;
M'ôter, pour faire bien, du grenier de céans
Cette longue lunette à faire peur aux gens,
Et cent brimborions dont l'aspect importune;
Ne point aller chercher ce qu'on fait dans la lune,
Et vous mêler un peu de ce qu'on fait chez vous,
Où nous voyons aller tout sens dessus dessous.

Act II Scene Seven

PHILAMINTE

"Womanly"! That world is old and crude.
It reeks, in fact, of its antiquity.

BÉLISE

It sounds old-fashioned and absurd to me.

CHRYSALE

See here; I can't contain myself; I mean
To drop the mask for once, and vent my spleen.
The whole world thinks you mad, and I am through—

PHILAMINTE

How's that, Sir?

CHRYSALE (*to Bélise*)

Sister, I am addressing *you*.
The least mistake in speech you can't forgive,
but how mistakenly you chose to live!
I'm sick of those eternal books you've got;
In my opinion, you should burn the lot,
Save for that Plutarch where I press my collars,
And leave the studious life to clerks and scholars;
And do throw out, if I may be emphatic,
That great long frightful spyglass in the attic,
And all these other gadgets, and do it soon.
Stop trying to see what's happening in the moon
And look what's happening in your household here,
Where everything around us upside down and queer.

Il n'est pas bien honnête, et pour beaucoup de causes,
Q'une femme étudie et sache tant de choses:
Former aux bonnes moeurs l'esprit de ses enfants,
Faire aller son ménage, avoir l'oeil sur ses gens[149],
Et régler la dépense avec économie,
Doit être son étude et sa philosophie.
Nos pères, sur ce point, étaient gens bien sensés,
Qui disaient qu'une femme en sait toujours assez
Quand la capacité de son esprit se hausse
A connaître un pourpoint d'avec un haut-de-chausse[159].
Les leurs ne lisaient point, mais elles vivaient bien;
Leurs ménages étaient tout leur docte entretien,
Et leurs livres, un dé, du fil et des aiguilles,
Dont elles travaillaient au trousseau de leurs filles.
Les femmes d'à présent sont bien loin de ces moeurs:
Elles veulent écrire et devenir auteur;
Nulle science n'est pour elles trop profonde,
Et céans beaucoup plus haut s'y laissent concevoir,
Et l'on sait tout chez moi, hors ce qu'il faut savoir.
On y sait comme[151] vont lune, étoile polaire,
Vénus, Saturne et Mars, dont je n'ai point affaire;
Et, dans ce vain savoir, qu'on va chercher si loin,
On ne sait comme va mon pot, dont j'ai besoin.
Mes gens à la science aspirent pour vous plaire,
Et tous ne font rien moins que[152] ce qu'ils ont à faire;
Raisonner est l'emploi de toute ma maison,
Et le raisonnement en bannit la raison[153].
L'un me brûle mon rôt en lisant quelque histoire,
L'autre rêve à des vers quand je demande à boire;
Enfin je vois par eux votre exemple suivi,
Et j'ai des serviteurs et ne suis point servi.
Une pauvre servante au moins m'était restée,
Qui de ce mauvais air n'était point infectée,
Et voilà qu'on la chasse avec un grand fracas
A cause qu'[154]elle manque à parler Vaugelas

For a hundred reasons, it's neither meet nor right
That a woman study and be erudite.
To teach her children manners, overlook
The household, train the servants and the cook,
And keep a thrifty budget—these should be
Her only study and philosophy.
Our fathers had a saying which made good sense:
A woman's polished her intelligence
Enough, they said, if she can pass the test
Of telling a pair of breeches from a vest.
Their wives read nothing, yet their lives were good;
Domestic lore was all they understood,
And all their books were needle and thread, with which
they made their daughters' trousseaus, stitch by stitch.
But women scorn such modest arts of late;
They want to scribble and to cogitate;
No mystery is too deep for them to plumb.
Is there a stranger house in Christendom
Than mine, where women are as mad as hatters,
And everything is known except what matters?
They know how Mars, the moon, and Venus turn,
And Saturn, too, that's none of my concern,
And what with all this vain and far-fetched learning,
They don't know if my roast of beef is burning.
My servants, who now aspire to culture, too,
Do anything but what they're paid to do;
Thinking is all this household thinks about,
And reasoning has driven reason out.
One spoils a sauce, while reading the dictionary;
One mumbles verses when I ask for sherry;
Because they ape the follies they've observed
In you, I keep six servants and am not served.
Just one poor wench remained who hadn't caught
The prevalent disease of lofty thought,
And now, since Vaugelas might find her lacking
In grammar, you've blown up and sent her packing.

Je vous le dis, ma soeur, tout ce train-là me blesse,
Car c'est, comme j'ai dit, à vous que je m'adresse.
Je n'aime point céans tous vos gens à latin,
Et principalement ce monsieur Trissotin.
C'est lui qui dans des vers vous a tympanisées[155];
Tous les propos qu'il tient sont des bilevesées[156]:
On cherche ce qu'il dit après qu'il a parlé;
Et je lui crois, pour moi, le timbre un peu fêlé[157].

PHILAMINTE

Quelle bassesse, ô ciel, et d'âme et de langage!

BÉLISE

Est-il de petits corps[158] un plus lourd assemblage,
Un esprit composé d'atomes plus bourgeois[159]?
Et de ce même sang se peut-il que je sois?
Je me veux mal de mort[169] d'être de votre race,
Et de confusion j'abandonne la place.

Sister (I'm speaking to you, as I said before),
These goings-on I censure and deplore.
I'm tired of visits from these pedants versed
In Latin, and that ass Trissotin's the worst.
He's flattered you in many a wretched sonnet;
There's a great swarm of queer bees in his bonnet;
Each time he speaks, one wonders what he's said;
I think, myself, that he's crazy in the head.

PHILAMINTE

Dear God, what brutishness of speech and mind!

BÉLISE

Could particles more grossly be combined,
Or atoms form an aggregate more crass?
And can we be of the same blood? Alas,
I hate myself because we two are kin,
And leave this scene in horror and chagrin.

Scène VIII

PHILAMINTE, CHRYSALE

———————

PHILAMINTE

Avez-vous à lâcher encore quelque trait?

CHRYSALE

Moi? Non. Ne parlons plus de querelle; c'est fait;
Discourons d'autre affaire. A votre fille aînée
On voit quelque dégoût pour les noeuds d'hyménée;
C'est une philosophe enfin, je n'en dis rien;
Elle est bien gouvernée, et vous faites fort bien.
Mais de tout autre humeur se trouve sa cadette,
Et je crois qu'il est bon de pourvoir Henriette,
De choisir un mari...

PHILAMINTE

              C'est à quoi j'ai songé,
Et je veux vous ouvrir l'intention que j'ai.
Ce monsieur Trissotin dont on vous fait un crime,
Et qui n'a pas l'honneur d'être dans votre estime,
Est celui que je prends pour l'époux qu'il lui faut,
Et je sais mieux que vous juger de ce qu'il vaut.
La contestation est ici superflue,
Et de tout point chez moi l'affaire est résolue.
Au moins ne dites mot du choix de cet époux:
Je veux à votre fille en parler avant vous.
J'ai des raisons à faire approuver ma conduite,
Et je connaîtrai bien si vous l'aurez instruite.

Scene Eight

PHILAMINTE, CHRYSALE

PHILAMINTE

Have you other shots to fire, or are you through?

CHRYSALE

I? No, no. No more quarreling. That will do.
Let's talk of something else. As we've heard her state,
Your eldest daughter scorns to take a mate.
She's a philosopher—mind you, I'm not complaining;
She's had the finest of maternal training.
But her younger sister's otherwise inclined,
And I've a notion that it's time to find
A match for Henriette—

PHILAMINTE

Exactly, and
I'll now inform you of the match I've planned.
That Trissotin whose visits you begrudge,
And whom you so contemptuously judge,
Is, I've decided, the appropriate man.
If you can't recognize his worth, I can.
Let's not discuss it; it's quite unnecessary;
I've thought things through; it's he whom she should marry.
Don't tell her of my choice, however; I choose
To be the first to let her know the news.
That she will listen to reason I have no doubt,
And if you seek to meddle, I'll soon find out.

Scène IX

ARISTE, CHRYSALE

———————

ARISTE

Hé bien? La femme[161] sort, mon frère, et je vois bien
Que vous venez d'avoir ensemble un entretien.

CHRYSALE

`Oui.

ARISTE

Quel est le succès[162]? Aurons-nous Henriette?
A-t-elle consenti? l'affaire est-elle faite?

CHRYSALE

Pas tout à fait encor.

ARISTE

Refuse-t-elle?

CHRYSALE

Non.

Scene Nine

ARISTE, CHRYSALE

ARISTE

Ah, Brother; your wife's just leaving, and it's clear
That you and she have had a conference here.

CHRYSALE

Yes.

ARISTE

Well, shall Clitandre have his Henriette?
Is your wife willing? Can the date be set?

CHRYSALE

Not altogether.

ARISTE

What, she refuses?

CHRYSALE

No.

ARISTE

Est-ce qu'elle balance?

CHRYSALE

En aucune façon.

ARISTE

Quoi donc?

CHRYSALE

C'est que pour gendre elle m'offre un autre homme.

ARISTE

Un autre homme pour gendre?

CHRYSALE

Un autre.

ARISTE

Qui se nomme?

CHRYSALE

Monsieur Trissotin.

ARISTE

Quoi! ce monsieur Trissotin ...

ARISTE

Is she wavering, then?

CHRYSALE

I wouldn't describe her so.

ARISTE

What, then?

CHRYSALE

There's someone else whom she prefers.

ARISTE

For a son-in-law?

CHRYSALE

Yes.

ARISTE

Who is this choice of hers?

CHRYSALE

Well... Trissotin.

ARISTE

What! That ass, that figure of fun—

CHRYSALE

Oui, qui parle toujours de vers et de latin.

ARISTE

Vous l'avez accepté?

CHRYSALE

Moi? Point, à Dieu ne plaise.

ARISTE

Qu'avez-vous répondu?

CHRYSALE

Rien; et je suis bien aise
De n'avoir point parlé, pour ne m'engager pas.

ARISTE

La raison est fort belle, et c'est faire un grand pas.
Avez-vous su du moins lui proposer Clitandre?

CHRYSALE

Non: car, comme j'ai vu qu'on parlait d'autre gendre,
J'ai cru qu'il était mieux de ne m'avancer point.

ARISTE

Certes, votre prudence est rare au dernier point!
N'avez-vous point de honte avec votre mollesse?
Et se peut-il qu'un homme ait assez de faiblesse
Pour laisser à sa femme un pouvoir absolu
Et n'oser attaquer ce qu'elle a résolu?

CHRYSALE

Who babbles verse and Latin? Yes, that's the one.

ARISTE

Did you agree to him?

CHRYSALE

I? No; God forbid!

ARISTE

What did you say, then?

CHRYSALE

   Nothing; and what I did
Was wise, I think, for it left me uncommitted.

ARISTE

I see! What strategy! How nimble-witted!
Did you, at least, suggest Clitandre, Brother?

CHRYSALE

No. When I found her partial toward another,
It seemed best not to push things then and there.

ARISTE

Your prudence, truly, is beyond compare!
Aren't you ashamed to be so soft and meek?
How can a man be so absurdly weak
As to yield his wife an absolute dominion
And never dare contest her least opinion?

CHRYSALE

Mon Dieu, vous en parlez, mon frère, bien à l'aise,
Et vous ne savez pas comme le bruit[163] me pèse.
J'aime fort le repos, la paix et la douceur,
Et ma femme est terrible avecque[164] son humeur.
Du nom de philosophe elle fait grand mystère[165],
Mais elle n'en est pas pour cela moins colère;
Et sa morale, faite à mépriser le bien[166],
Sur l'aigreur de sa bile opère comme rien.
Pour peu que l'on s'oppose à ce que veut sa tête,
On en a pour huit jours d'effroyable tempête.
Elle me fait trembler dès qu'elle prend son ton;
Je ne sais où me mettre, et c'est un vrai dragon.
Et cependant, avec toute se diablerie,
Il faut que je l'appelle et mon coeur et ma mie.

ARISTE

Allez, c'est se moquer. Votre femme, entre nous,
Est, par vos lachetés, souveraine sur vous.
Son pouvoir n'est fondé que sur votre faiblesse;
C'est de vous qu'elle prend le titre de maîtresse;
Vous-même à ses hauteurs vous vous abandonnez,
Et vous faites mener, en bête[167], par le nez.
Quoi! vous ne pouvez pas, voyant comme on vous nomme[168],
Vous résoudre une fois à vouloir être un homme,
A faire condescendre une femme à vos voeux
Et prendre assez de coeur pour un: Je le veux?
Vous laisserez sans honte immoler[169] votre fille
Aux folles visions qui tiennent la famille,
Et de tout votre bien revêtir un nigaud
Pour six mots qu'il leur fait sonner haut,
Un pédant qu'à tout coup[170] votre femme apostrophe
Du nom de bel esprit et de grand philosophe,

CHRYSALE

Ah, Brother, that's easy enough for you to say.
You've no idea how noisy quarrels weigh
Upon my heart, which loves tranquillity,
And how my wife's bad temper frightens me.
Her nature's philosophic—or that's her claim,
But her tongue's sharp and savage all the same;
All this uplifting thought has not decreased
Her rancorous behavior in the least.
If I cross her even slightly, she will loose
An eight-day howling tempest of abuse.
There's no escape from her consuming ire;
She's like some frightful dragon spitting fire;
And yet, despite her devilish ways, my fear
Obliges me to call her "pet" and "dear."

ARISTE

For shame. That's nonsense. It's your cowardice
Which lets your wife rule over you like this.
What power she has, your weakness has created;
She only rules because you've abdicated;
She couldn't bully you unless you chose,
Like an ass, to let her lead you by the nose.
Come now: despite your timid nature, can
You not resolve for once to be a man,
And, saying "This is how it's going to be,"
Lay down the law, and make your wife agree?
Shall you sacrifice your Henriette to these
Besotted women and their fantasies,
And take for son-in-law, and *heir*, a fool
who's turned your house into a Latin school,
A pedant whom your dazzled wife extols
As best of wits, most erudite of souls

127

D'homme qu'en vers galants jamais on n'égala,
Et qui n'est, comme on sait, rien moins que tout cela?
Allez, encore un coup, c'est une moquerie,
Et votre lâcheté mérite qu'on en rie.

CHRYSALE

Oui, vous avez raison, et je vois que j'ai tort.
Allons, il faut enfin montrer un coeur plus fort,
Mon frère.

ARISTE

C'est bien dit.

CHRYSALE

C'est une chose infâme
Que d'être si soumis au pouvoir d'une femme.

ARISTE

Fort bien.

CHRYSALE

De ma douceur elle a trop profité.

ARISTE

Il est vrai.

CHRYSALE

Trop joui de ma facilité.

and peerless fashioner of galant verse,
And who, in all respects, could not be worse?
Once more I say, for shame: it's ludicrous
To see a husband cringe and cower thus.

CHRYSALE

Yes, you're quite right; I see that I've been wrong.
It's high time, Brother, to be firm and strong,
To take a stand.

ARISTE

Well said.

CHRYSALE

It's base, I know,
To let a woman dominate one so.

ARISTE

Quite right.

CHRYSALE

She's taken advantage of my patience.

ARISTE

She has.

CHRYSALE

And of my peaceful inclinations.

ARISTE

Sans doute.

CHRYSALE

Et je lui veux faire aujourd'hui connaître
Que ma fille est ma fille, et que j'en suis maître,
Pour lui prendre mari qui soit selon mes voeux.

ARISTE

Vous voilà raisonnable et comme je vous veux.

CHRYSALE

Vous êtes pour Clitandre, et savez sa demeure:
Faites-le-moi venir, mon frère, tout à l'heure.

ARISTE

J'y cours tout de ce pas.

CHRYSALE

C'est souffrir trop longtemps,
Et je m'en vais être homme à la barbe des gens[171].

ARISTE

That's true.

CHRYSALE

But, as she'll learn this very day,
My daughter's mine, and I shall have my way
And wed her to a man who pleases me.

ARISTE

Now you're the master, as I'd have you be.

CHRYSALE

Brother, as young Clitandre's spokesman, you
Know where to find him. Send him to me, do.

ARISTE

I'll go this instant.

CHRYSALE

Too long my will's been crossed;
Henceforth I'll be a man, whatever the cost.

Act III

Scène I

PHILAMINTE, ARMANDE, BÉLISE, TRISSOTIN, LÉPINE

PHILAMINTE

Ah! mettons-nous ici pour écouter à l'aise
Ces vers que mot à mot il est besoin qu'on pèse.

ARMANDE

Je brûle[172] de les voir.

BÉLISE

Et l'on s'en meurt chez nous.

PHILAMINTE (à *Trissotin*)

Ce sont charmes pour moi que ce qui part de vous.

ARMANDE

Ce m'est une douceur à nulle autre pareille.

BÉLISE

Ce sont repas friands qu'on donne à mon oreille.

Scene One

PHILAMINTE, ARMANDE, BÉLISE, TRISSOTIN, LÉPINE

PHILAMINTE

Let's all sit down and savor, thought by thought,
The verses which our learnèd guest has brought.

ARMANDE

I burn to see them.

BÉLISE

Yes; our souls are panting.

PHILAMINTE (*to Trissotin*)

All that your mind brings forth, I find enchanting.

ARMANDE

For me, your compositions have no peer.

BÉLISE

Their music is a banquet to my ear.

PHILAMINTE

Ne faites point languir de si pressants désirs.

ARMANDE

Dépêchez.

BÉLISE

Faites tôt, et hâtez nos plaisirs.

PHILAMINTE

A notre impatience offrez votre épigramme.

TRISSOTIN (*à Philaminte*)

Hélas![173] c'est un enfant tout nouveau-né, madame.
Son sort assurément a lieu de vous toucher,
Et c'est dans votre cour que j'en viens d'accoucher[174].

PHILAMINTE

Pour me le rendre cher, il suffit de son père.

TRISSOTIN

Votre approbation lui peut servir de mère.

BÉLISE

Qu'il a d'esprit!

PHILAMINTE

Don't tantilize your breathless audience.

ARMANDE

Do hurry—

BÉLISE

And relieve this sweet suspense.

PHILAMINTE

Yield to our urging; give us your epigram.

TRISSOTIN (*to Philaminte*)

Madam, 'tis but an infant; still, I am
In hopes that you may condescend to love it,
Since on your doorstep I was delivered of it.

PHILAMINTE

Knowing its father, I can do no other.

TRISSOTIN

Your kind approval, then, shall be its mother.

BÉLISE

What wit he has!

Scène II

HENRIETTE, PHILAMINTE, ARMANDE, BÉLISE, TRISSOTIN, LÉPINE

———————

PHILAMINTE
(*à Henriette, qui veut se retirer*)

Holà! pourquoi donc fuyez-vous?

HENRIETTE

C'est de peur de troubler un entretien si doux.

PHILAMINTE

Approchez, et venez de toutes vos oreilles
Prendre part au plaisir d'entendre des merveilles.

HENRIETTE

Je sais peu les beautés de tout ce qu'on écrit,
Et ce n'est pas mon fait que les choses d'esprit.

PHILAMINTE

Il n'importe. Aussi bien ai-je à vous dire ensuite
Un secret dont il faut que vous soyez instruite.

TRISSOTIN (*à Henriette*)

Les sciences[175] n'ont rien qui puissent enflammer,
Et vous ne vous piquez que de savoir charmer.

Scene Two

HENRIETTE, PHILAMINTE, ARMANDE, BÉLISE, TRISSOTIN, LÉPINE

PHILAMINTE
(to Henriette, who has entered and has turned at once to go)

Ho! Don't rush off like that.

HENRIETTE

I feared I might disrupt your pleasant chat.

PHILAMINTE

Come here, and pay attention, and you shall share
The joy of hearing something rich and rare.

HENRIETTE

I'm no fit judge of elegance in letters;
I leave such heady pastimes to my betters.

PHILAMINTE

That doesn't matter. Stay, and when we're through
I shall reveal a sweet surprise to you.

TRISSOTIN *(to Henriette)*

What need you know of learning and the arts,
Who know so well the way to charm men's hearts?

HENRIETTE

Aussi peu l'un que l'autre; et je n'ai nulle envie ...

BÉLISE

Ah! songeons à l'enfant nouveau-né, je vous prie.

PHILAMINTE (*à Lépine*)

Allons, petit garçon, vite de quoi s'asseoir.
(*Le laquais tombe avec la chaise)*
Voyez l'impertinent[176]! Est-ce que l'on doit choir,
Après avoir appris l'équilibre des choses?

BÉLISE

De ta chute, ignorant, ne vois-tu pas les causes,
Et qu'elle vient d'avoir du point fixe écarté
Ce que nous appelons centre de gravité?

LÉPINE

Je m'en suis aperçu, madame, étant par terre.

PHILAMINTE (*à Lépine qui sort*)

Le lourdaud!

TRISSOTIN

Bien lui prend[177] de n'être pas de verre.

ARMANDE

Ah! de l'esprit partout!

HENRIETTE

Sir, I know neither; nor is it my ambition—

BÉLISE

Oh, please! Let's hear the infant composition.

PHILAMINTE (*to Lépine*)

Quick, boy, some chairs.
   (*Lépine falls down in bringing a chair*)
            Dear God, how loutish! Ought you
To fall like that, considering what we've taught you
Regarding equilibrium and its laws?

BÉLISE

Look what you've done, fool. Surely you see the cause?
It was by wrongly shifting what we call
The center of gravity, that you came to fall.

LÉPINE

I saw that when I hit the floor, alas.

PHILAMINTE (*to Lépine, as he leaves*)

Dolt!

TRISSOTIN

It's a blessing he's not made of glass.

ARMANDE

What wit! It never falters!

BÉLISE

Cela ne tarit pas.

PHILAMINTE

Servez-nous promptement votre aimable repas.

TRISSOTIN

Pour cette grande faim qu'à mes yeux on expose
Un plat seul de huit vers me semble peu de chose,
Et je pense qu'ici je ne ferai pas mal
De joindre à l'épigramme, ou bien au madrigal[178],
Le ragoût[179] d'un sonnet, qui chez une princesse
A passé pour avoir quelque délicatesse.
Il est de sel attique[180] assaisonné partout,
Et vous le trouverez, je crois, d'assez bon goût.

ARMANDE

Ah! je n'en doute point.

PHILAMINTE

Donnons vite audience.

BÉLISE (*à chaque fois qu'il veut lire, l'interrompt*)

Je sens d'aise à mon coeur tressaillir par avance.
J'aime la poésie avec entêtement[181],
Et surtout quand les vers sont tournés galamment.

BÉLISE

Not in the least.

PHILAMINTE

Now then, do serve us your poetic feast.

TRISSOTIN

For such great hunger as confronts me here,
An eight-line dish would not suffice, I fear.
My epigram's too slight. It would be wiser,
I think, to give you first, as appetizer,
A sonnet which a certain princess found
Subtle in sense, delectable in sound.
I've seasoned it with Attic salt throughout,
And you will find it tasty, I have no doubt.

ARMANDE

How could we not?

PHILAMINTE

Let's listen, with concentration.

BÉLISE (*interrupting Trissotin each time he starts to read*)

My heart is leaping with anticipation.
I'm mad for poetry, and I love it best
When pregnant thoughts are gallantly expressed.

PHILAMINTE

Si nous parlons toujours, il ne pourra rien dire.

TRISSOTIN

SO ...

BÉLISE (*à Henriette*)

Silence, ma nièce...

ARMANDE

Ah! laissez-le donc lire.

TRISSOTIN

SONNET A LA PRINCESSE URANIE[182]
SUR SA FIEVRE
Votre prudence est endormie,
De traiter magnifiquement
Et de loger superbement
Votre plus cruelle ennemie.

BELISE

Ah! le joli début!

ARMANDE

Qu'il a le tour galant!

PHILAMINTE

Lui seul des vers aisés possède le talent!

PHILAMINTE

So long as we talk, our guest can't say a word.

TRISSOTIN

SO—

BÉLISE (*to Henriette*)

Niece, be silent.

ARMANDE

Please! Let the poem be heard.

TRISSOTIN

SONNET TO THE PRINCESS URANIE, REGARDNG HER FEVER

Your prudence, Madam, must have drowsed
When you took in so hot a foe
And let him be so nobly housed,
And feasted and regaled him so.

BÉLISE

A fine first quatrain!

ARMANDE

And the style! How gallant!

PHILAMINTE

For metric flow he has a matchless talent.

ARMANDE

A "prudence endormie" il faut rendre les armes.

BÉLISE

"Loger son ennemie" est pour moi plein de charme.

PHILAMINTE

J'aime "superbement" et "magnifiquement";
Ces deux adverbes joints font admirablement.

BÉLISE

Prêtons l'oreille au reste.

TRISSOTIN

Votre prudence endormie,
De traiter magnifiquement
Et de loger superbement
Votre plus belle ennemie.

ARMANDE

"Prudence endormie!"

BÉLISE

"Loger son ennemie"

PHILAMINTE

"Superbement" et "magnifiquement!"

ARMANDE

"Your *prudence* must have *drowsed*": a charming touch.

BÉLISE

"So hot a foe" delights me quite as much.

PHILAMINTE

I think that "feasted and regaled" conveys
A sense of richness in so many ways.

BÉLISE

Let's listen to the rest.

TRISSOTIN

Your prudence, Madam, must have drowsed
When you took in so hot a foe
And let him be so nobly housed,
And feasted and regaled him so.

ARMANDE

"Your prudence must have drowsed!"

BÉLISE

"So hot a foe!"

PHILAMINTE

"Feasted and regaled!"

TRISSOTIN

Faites-la sortir, quoi qu'on die[183],
De votre riche appartement[184],
Où cette ingrate insolemment
Attaque votre belle vie.

BÉLISE

Ah! tout doux, laissez-moi, de grâce, respirer.

ARMANDE

Donnez-nous, s'il vous plaît, le loisir d'admirer.

PHILAMINTE

On se sent, à ces vers, jusques au fond de l'âme
Couler je ne sais quoi qui fait que l'on se pâme.

ARMANDE

"Faites-la sortir, quoi qu'on die,
De votre riche appartement."
Que "riche appartement" est là joliment dit!
Et que la métaphore est mise avec esprit!

PHILAMINTE

"Faites-la sortie, quoi qu'on die."
Ah! que ce "quoi qu'on die" est d'un goût admirable!
C'est, à mon sentiment, un endroit impayable[185].

TRISSOTIN

Say what they may, the wretch must go!
From your rich lodging drive away
This ingrate who, as well you know,
Would make your precious life his prey.

BÉLISE

Oh! Pause a moment, I beg you; one is breathless.

ARMANDE

Let us digest those verses, which are deathless.

PHILAMINTE

There's a rare something in those lines which captures
One's inmost heart, and stirs the soul to raptures.

ARMANDE

"Say what thay may, the wretch must go!
    From your rich lodging away..."
How apt that is—"rich lodging." I adore
The wit and freshness of that metaphor!

PHILAMINTE

"Say what they may, the wretch must go!"
That "Say what they may" is greatly to my liking.
I've never encountered any words more striking.

ARMANDE

De "quoi qu'on die" aussi mon coeur est amoureux.

BÉLISE

Je suis de votre avis, "quoi qu'on die" est heureux.

ARMANDE

Je voudrais l'avoir fait.

BÉLISE

Il vaut toute une pièce.

PHILAMINTE

Mais en comprend-on bien comme moi la finesse?

ARMANDE et BÉLISE

Oh! oh!

PHILAMINTE

"Faites-la sortie, quoi qu'on die."
Que de la fièvre on prenne ici les intérêts;
N'ayez aucun égard, moquez-vous des caquets[186],
    "Faites-la sortir, quoi qu'on die,
    Quoi qu'on die, quoi qu'on die!"
Ce "quoi qu'on die" en dit beaucoup plus qu'il ne semble.
Je ne sais pas, pour moi, si chacun me ressemble,
Mais j'entends là-dessous un million de mots.

ARMANDE

Nor I. That "Say what they may" bewitches me.

BÉLISE

"Say what they may" is brilliant, I agree.

ARMANDE

Oh, to have said it.

BÉLISE

It's a whole poem in a phrase.

PHILAMINTE

But have you fully grasped what it conveys,
As I have?

ARMANDE and BÉLISE

Oh! Oh!

PHILAMINTE

"Say what they may, the wretch must go"!
That means, if people take the fever's side,
Their pleading should be scornfully denied.
    "Say what they may, the wretch must go,
    Say what they may, say what they may"!
There's more in that "Say what they may" than first appears.
Perhaps I am alone in this, my dears,
But I see no limit to what that phrase implies.

LES FEMMES SAVANTES

BÉLISE

Il est vrai qu'il dit plus de choses qu'il n'est gros.

PHILAMINTE (*à Trissotin*)

Mais, quand vous avez fait ce charmant "quoi qu'on die",
Avez-vous compris, vous, toute son énergie?
Songiez-vous bien vous-même à tout ce qu'il nous dit,
Et pensiez-vous alors y mettre tant d'esprit?

TRISSOTIN

Hai! hai!

ARMANDE

  J'ai fort aussi "l'ingrate" dans la tête,
Cette ingrate de fièvre, injuste, malhonnête,
Qui traite mal les gens qui la loge chez eux.

PHILAMINTE

Enfin les quatrains sont admirables tous deux.
Venons-en promptement aux tiercets[187], je vous prie.

ARMANDE

Ah! s'il vous plaît, encore une fois "quoi qu'on die".

TRISSOTIN

Faites-la sortir, quoi qu'on die ...

PHILAMINTE, ARMANDE et BELISE

"Quoi qu'on die!"

BÉLISE

It's true, it means a great deal for its size.

PHILAMINTE (*to Trissotin*)

Sir, when you wrote this charming "Say what they may,"
Did you know your own great genius? Can you say
That you were conscious, then, of all the wit
And wealth of meaning we have found it it?

TRISSOTIN

Ah! Well!

ARMANDE

I'm very fond of "ingrate," too.
It well describes that villain fever, who
Repays his hosts by causing them distress.

PHILAMINTE

In short, the quatrains are a great success.
Do let us have the tercets now, I pray.

ARMANDE

Oh, please, let's once more hear "Say what they may."

TRISSOTIN

Say what they may, the wretch must go!

PHILAMINTE, ARMANDE, and BÉLISE

"Say what they may!"

TRISSOTIN

De votre riche appartement...

PHILAMINTE, ARMANDE et BÉLISE

"Riche appartement!"

TRISSOTIN

Où cette ingrate insolemment ...

PHILAMINTE, ARMANDE et BÉLISE

Cette "ingrate" de fièvre!

TRISSOTIN

Attaque votre belle vie.

PHILAMINTE

"Votre belle vie!"

ARMANDE et BÉLISE

Ah!

TRISSOTIN

Quoi! sans respecter votre rang,
Elle se prend[188] à votre sang ...

PHILAMINTE, ARMANDE et BÉLISE

Ah!

Act III   Scene Two

TRISSOTIN

From your rich lodging drive away...

PHILAMINTE, ARMANDE, and BÉLISE

"Rich lodging!"

TRISSOTIN

This ingrate who, as well you know...

PHILAMINTE, ARMANDE, and BÉLISE

That "ingrate" of a fever!

TRISSOTIN

Would make your precious life his prey.

PHILAMINTE

"Your precious life!"

ARMANDE and BÉLISE

Ah!

TRISSOTIN

What! Shall he mock your rank, and pay
No deference to the blood of kings?

PHILAMINTE, ARMANDE, and BÉLISE

Ah!

TRISSOTIN

Et nuit et jour vous fait outrage!
Si vous la conduisez aux bains,
Sans la marchander[189] davantage,
Noyez-la de vos propres mains.

PHILAMINTE

On n'en peut plus.

BÉLISE

On pâme.

ARMANDE

On se meurt de plaisir.

PHILAMINTE

De mille doux frissons vous vous sentez saisir.

ARMANDE

"Si vous la conduisez au bains ..."

BÉLISE

"Sans la marchander davantage ..."

PHILAMINTE

"Noyez-la de vos propres mains."
De vos propres mains, là, noyez-la dans les bains.

TRISSOTIN

Shall he afflict you night and day,
And shall you tolerate such things?
No! To the baths you must repair,
And with your own hands drown him there.

PHILAMINTE

I'm overcome.

BÉLISE

I'm faint.

ARMANDE

I'm ravished, quite.

PHILAMINTE

One feels a thousand tremors of delight.

ARMANDE

"And shall you tolerate such things?"

BÉLISE

"No! To the bath you must repair..."

PHILAMINTE

"And with our own hands drown him there."
Drown him, that is to say, in the bath-water.

ARMANDE

Chaque pas dans vos vers rencontre un trait charmant.

BÉLISE

Partout on s'y promène avec ravissement.

PHILAMINTE

On n'y saurait marcher que sur les belles choses.

ARMANDE

Ce sont petits chemins tout parsemés de roses.

TRISSOTIN

Le sonnet donc vous semble ...

PHILAMINTE

Admirable, nouveau,
Et personne jamais n'a rien fait de si beau.

BÉLISE (*à Henriette*)

Quoi! sans émotion pendant cette lecture!
Vous faites là, ma nièce, une étrange figure.

HENRIETTE

Chacun fait ici bas la figure qu'il peut,
Ma tante, et bel esprit, il ne l'est pas qui veut.

Act III Scene Two

ARMANDE

Your verse, at each step, gives some glad surprise.

BÉLISE

Wherever one turns, fresh wonders greet the eyes.

PHILAMINTE

One treads on beauty, wandering through your lines.

ARMANDE

They're little paths all strewn with eglantines.

TRISSOTIN

You find the poem, then—

PHILAMINTE

      Perfect, and, what's more,
Novel: the like was never done before.

BÉLISE (*to Henriette*)

What, Niece, did not this reading stir your heart?
By saying nothing, you've played a dreary part.

HENRIETTE

We play what parts we're given, here below;
Wishing to be a wit won't make one so.

TRISSOTIN

Peut-être que mes vers importunent madame.

HENRIETTE

Point: je n'écoute pas.

PHILAMINTE

Ah! voyons l'épigramme.

TRISSOTIN

SUR UN CARROSSE DE COULEUR AMARANTE
DONNÉ À UNE DAME DE SES AMIES.[190]

PHILAMINTE

Ses titres ont toujours quelque chose de rare.

ARMANDE

A cent beaux traits d'esprit leur nouveauté prépare.

TRISSOTIN

L'amour si chèrement m'a vendu son lien ...

PHILAMINTE, ARMANDE et BÉLISE

Ah!

TRISSOTIN

Qu'il m'en coûte déjà la moitié de mon bien;
  Et, quand tu vois ce beau carrosse,
  Où tant d'or se révèle en bosse
  Qu'il étonne tout le pays
  Et fait pompeusement triompher ma Laïs,[191]....

TRISSOTIN

Perhaps my verses bored her.

HENRIETTE

No indeed; I didn't listen.

PHILAMINTE

The epigram! Please proceed.

TRISSOTIN

CONCERNING A VERMILION COACH, GIVEN
TO A LADY OF HIS ACQUAINTANCE...

PHILAMINTE

There's always something striking about his titles.

ARMANDE

They ready us for the wit of his recitals.

TRISSOTIN

Love sells his bonds to me at such a rate...

PHILAMINTE, ARMANDE, and BÉLISE

Ah!

TRISSOTIN

I've long since spent the half of my estate;
    And when you see this coach, embossed
  With heavy gold at such a cost
  That all the dazzled countryside
    Gapes as my Laïs passes in her pride...

PHILAMINTE

Ah! ma Laïs! Voilà de l'érudition.

BÉLISE

L'enveloppe[192] est jolie et vaut un million.

TRISSOTIN

Et, quand tu vois ce beau carrosse
Ou tant d'or se relève en bosse
Qu'il étonne tout le pays
Et fait pompeusement triompher ma Laïs,
Ne dis plus qu'il est amarante,
Dis plutôt qu'il est de ma rente.

ARMANDE

Oh! oh! oh! Celui-là ne s'attend point du tout.

PHILAMINTE

On n'a que lui qui puisse écrire de ce goût.

BÉLISE

"Ne dis plus qu'il est amarante,
Dis plutôt qu'il est de ma rente."
Voilà qui se décline[193]:
"Ma rente, de ma rente, à ma rente."

PHILAMINTE

Listen to that. "My Laïs." How erudite!

BÉLISE

A stunning reference. So exactly right.

TRISSOTIN

And when you see this coach, embossed
With heavy gold at such cost
That all the dazzled countryside
Gapes as my Laïs passes in her pride,
Know by that vision of vermilion
That what was mine is now *her* million.

ARMANDE

Oh! Oh! I didn't foresee that final twist.

PHILAMINTE

We have no subtler epigrammatist.

BÉLISE

"Know by that vision of vermilion
That what was mine is now *her* million."
The rhyme is clever, and yet not forced:
"*ver*million, *her* million."

PHILAMINTE

Je ne sais, du moment que je vous ai connu,
Si sur votre sujet j'eus l'esprit prévenu[194],
Mais j'admire partout vos vers et votre prose.

TRISSOTIN (*à Philaminte*)

Si vous vouliez de vous nous montrer quelque chose,
A notre tour aussi nous pourrions admirer.

PHILAMINTE

Je n'ai rien fait en vers, mais j'ai lieu d'espérer
Que je pourrai bientôt vous montrer, en amie,
Huit chapitres du plan de notre académie.
Platon[195] s'est au projet simplement arrêté,
Quand de sa République il a fait le traité;
Mais à l'effet entier je veux pousser l'idée
Que j'ai sur le papier en prose accomodée:
Car enfin je me sens un étrange dépit
Du tort que l'on nous fait du côté de l'esprit;
Et je veux nous venger, toutes tant que nous sommes,
De cette indigne classe où nous rangent les hommes
De borner[196] nos talents à des futilités
Et nous fermer la porte aux sublimes clarté.[197]

ARMANDE

C'est faire à notre sexe une trop grande offense
De n'étendre l'effort de notre intelligence
Qu'à juger d'une jupe et de l'air d'un manteau,
Ou des beautés d'un point, ou d'un brocart nouveau.

PHILAMINTE

Since first we met, Sir, I have had the highest
Opinion of you; it may be that I'm biased;
But all you write, to my mind, stands alone.

TRISSOTIN (*to Philaminte*)

If you'd but read us something of your own,
One might reciprocate your admiration.

PHILAMINTE

I've no new poems, but it's my expectation
That soon, in some eight chapters, you may see
The plans I've made for our Academy.
Plato, in his *Republic*, did not go
Beyond an abstract outline, as you know,
But what I've shaped in words, I shall not fail
To realize, in most concrete detail.
I'm much offended by the disrespect
Which men display for women's intellect,
And I intend to avenge us, every one,
For all the slighting things which men have done—
Assigning us to care which stunt our souls,
And banning our pursuit of studious goals.

ARMANDE

It's too insulting to forbid our sex
To ponder any questions more complex
Than whether some lace is pretty, or some brocade,
And whether a skirt or cloak is nicely made.

BÉLISE

Il faut se relever de ce honteux partage,
Et mettre hautement notre esprit hors de page[198].

TRISSOTIN

Pour les dames on sait mon respect en tous lieux;
Et, si je rends hommage aux brillants de leurs yeux,
De leur esprit aussi j'honore les lumières.

PHILAMINTE

Le sexe aussi vous rend justice en ces matières;
Mais nous voulons montrer à de certains esprits,
Dont l'orgueilleux savoir nous traite avec mépris,
Que de sciences aussi les femmes sont meublées;
Qu'on peut faire comme eux de doctes assemblées,
Conduites par cela par des ordres meilleurs[199];
Qu'on y veut réunir ce qu'on sépare ailleurs[200],
Mêler le beau langage et les hautes sciences,
Découvrir la nature en mille expériences,
Et, sur les questions qu'on pourra poser,
Faire entrer chaque secte et n'en point épouser.

TRISSOTIN

Je m'attache, pour l'ordre, au péripatétisme[201].

PHILAMINTE

Pour les abstactions j'aime le platonisme[202].

BÉLISE

It's time we broke our mental chains, and stated
Our high intent to be emancipated.

TRISSOTIN

My deep respect for women none can deny;
Though I may praise a lady's lustrous eye,
I honor, too, the lustre of her mind.

PHILAMINTE

For that, you have the thanks of womankind;
But there are some proud scholars I could mention
To whom we'll prove, despite their condescension,
That women may be learnèd if they please,
And found, like men, their own academies.
Ours, furthermore, shall be more wisely run
Than theirs; we'll roll all disciplines into one.
Uniting letters, in a rich alliance,
With all the tools and theories of science,
And in our thought refusing to be thrall
To any school, but making use of all.

TRISSOTIN

For method, Aristotle suits me well.

PHILAMINTE

But in abstractions, Plato *does* excel.

ARMANDE

Epicure[203] me plaît, et ses dogmes sont forts.

BÉLISE

Je m'accommode assez, pour moi, des petits corps;
Mais le vide à souffrir me semble difficile,
Et je goûte bien mieux la matière subtile.

TRISSOTIN

Descartes[204], pour l'aimant, donne fort dans mon sens.

ARMANDE

J'aime ses tourbillons.

PHILAMINTE

Moi, ses mondes tombants.

ARMANDE

Il me tarde de voir notre assemblée ouverte
Et de nous signaler par quelque découverte.

TRISSOTIN

On en attend beaucoup de vos vives clartés,
Et pour vous la nature a peu d'obscurités.

PHILAMINTE

Pour moi, sans me flatter, j'en ai déjà fait une,
Et j'ai vu clairement des hommes dans la lune[205].

ARMANDE

The thought of Epicurus is very keen.

BÉLISE

I rather like his atoms, but as between
A vacuum and a field of subtle matter
I find it easier to accept the latter.

TRISSOTIN

On magnetism, Descartes supports my notions.

ARMANDE

I love his falling worlds...

PHILAMINTE

And whirling motions!

ARMANDE

I can't wait for our conclaves. We shall proclaim
Discoveries, and they shall bring us fame.

TRISSOTIN

Yes, to your keen minds Nature can but yield,
And let her rarest secrets be revealed.

PHILAMINTE

I can already offer one such rarity:
I have seen men in the moon, with perfect clarity.

BÉLISE

Je n'ai point encor vu d'hommes, comme je crois;
Mais j'ai vu des clochers tout comme je vous vois.

ARMANDE

Nous appronfondirons, ainsi que la physique,
Grammaire, histoire, vers, morale et politique.

PHILAMINTE

La morale a des traits dont mon coeur est épris,
Et c'était autrefois l'amour des grands esprits;
Mais aux stoïciens je donne l'avantage,
Et je ne trouve rien de si beau que leur sage[206].

ARMANDE

Pour la langue on verra dans peu nos règlements,
Et nous y prétendrons faire des remuements[207],
Par une antipathie, ou juste ou naturelle[208],
Nous avons pris chacune une haine mortelle
Pour un nombre de mots, soit ou verbes ou noms,
Que mutuellement nous nous abandonnons[209];
Contre eux nous préparons de mortelles sentences,
Et nous devons ouvrir nos doctes conférences
Par les proscriptions de tous ces mots divers
Dont nous voulons purger et la prose et les vers.

PHILAMINTE

Mais le plus beau projet de notre académie,
Une entreprise noble et dont je suis ravie,
Un dessein plein de gloire, et qui sera vanté
Chez tous les beaux esprits de la prospérité,

BÉLISE

I'm not sure I've seen men, but I can say
That I've seen steeples there, as plain as day.

ARMANDE

To master grammar and physics is our intent,
And history, ethics, verse and government.

PHILAMINTE

Ethics, which thrills me in so many respects,
Was once the passion of great intellects;
But it's the Stoics to whom I'd give the prize;
They knew that only the virtuous can be wise.

ARMANDE

Regarding language, we aim to renovate
Our tongue through laws which soon we'll promulgate.
Each of us has conceived a hatred, based
On outraged reason or offended taste,
For certain nouns and verbs. We've gathered these
Into a list of shared antipathies,
And shall proceed to doom and banish them.
At each of our learned gatherings, we'll condemn
In mordant terms those words which we propose
To purge from usage, whether in verse or prose.

PHILAMINTE

But our academy's noblest plan of action,
A scheme in which I take deep satisfaction,
A glorious project which will earn the praise
Of all discerning minds of future days,

C'est le retranchement de ces syllabes sales
Qui dans les plus beaux mots produisent des scandales,
Ces jouets éternels des sots de tous les temps,
Ces fades lieux communs de nos méchants plaisants,
Ces sources d'un amas d'équivoques infâmes
Dont on vient faire insulte à la pudeur des femmes.

TRISSOTIN

Voilà certainement d'admirables projets!

BÉLISE

Vous verrez nos statuts quand ils seront tous faits.

TRISSOTIN

Ils ne sauraient manquer d'être tous beaux et sages.

ARMANDE

Nous serons par nos lois les juges des ouvrages.
Par nos lois, proses et vers, tout sera soumis:
Nul n'aura de l'esprit, hors nous et nos amis.
Nous chercherons partout à trouver à redire,
Et ne verrons que nous qui sache bien écrire[210].

Is to suppress those *syllables* which, though found
In blameless words, may have a shocking sound,
Which naughty punsters utter with a smirk,
Which, age on age, coarse jesters overwork,
And which, by filthy double meanings, vex
the finer feelings of the female sex.

TRISSOTIN

You have most wondrous plans, beyond a doubt!

BÉLISE

You'll see our by-laws, once we've worked them out.

TRISSOTIN

They can't fail to be beautiful and wise.

ARMANDE

By our high standards we shall criticize
Whatever's written, and be severe with it.
We'll show that only we and our friends have wit.
We'll search out faults in everything, while citing
Ourselves alone for pure and flawless writing.

Scène III

LÉPINE, TRISSOTIN, BÉLISE, ARMANDE, PHILAMINTE, HENRIETTE, VADIUS

LÉPINE (*à Trissotin*)

Monsieur, un homme est là qui veut parler à vous.
Il est vêtu de noir et parle d'un ton doux.
    (*Tous se lèvent*)

TRISSOTIN

C'est cet ami savant qui m'a fait tant d'insistance.
De lui donner l'honneur de votre connaissance.

PHILAMINTE

Pour le faire venir vous avez tout crédit.
(*A Armande et à Bélise*)
Faisons bien les honneurs au moins de notre esprit.
(*A Henriette qui s'en va*)
Holà! je vous ai dit en paroles bien claires
Que j'ai besoin de vous.

HENRIETTE

Mais pour quelles affaires?

Scene Three

LÉPINE, TRISSOTIN, PHILAMINTE, BÉLISE, ARMANDE, HENRIETTE, VADIUS

———————————

LÉPINE (*To Trissotin*)

There's a man outside to see you, Sir; he's wearing
Black, and he has a gentle voice and bearing.
    (*all rise*)

TRISSOTIN

It's that learnèd friend of mine, who's begged me to
Procure for him the honor of meeting you.

PHILAMINTE

Please have him enter; you have our full consent.
    (*Trissotin goes to admit Vadius; Philaminte
        speaks to Armande and Bélise.*)
We must be gracious, and *most* intelligent.
    (*To Henriette, who seeks to leave*)
Whoa, there! I told you plainly, didn't I,
That I wished you to remain with us?

HENRIETTE

But why?

PHILAMINTE

Venez, on va dans peu vous les faire savoir.

TRISSOTIN (*se tournant vers Vadius*)

Voici l'homme qui meurt du désir de vous voir.
En vous le produisant[211], je ne crains point le blâme
D'avoir admis chez vous un profane, madame:
Il peut tenir son coin[212] parmi les beaux esprits.

PHILAMINTE

La main qui le présente en dit assez le prix.

TRISSOTIN

Il a des vieux auteurs la pleine intelligence
Et sait du grec, madame, autant qu'homme de France.

PHILAMINTE (*à Bélise*)

Du grec! ô ciel! du grec! Il sait du grec, ma soeur!

BELISE (*à Armande*)

Ah! ma nièce, du grec!

ARMANDE

Du grec! quelle douceur!

PHILAMINTE

Quoi! monsieur sait du grec! Ah! permettez, de grâce,
Que, pour l'amour du grec, monsieur, on vous embrasse.
(Il les baise toutes, jusques à Henriette, qui le refuse.)

PHILAMINTE

Come back, and you shall shortly understand.

TRISSOTIN (*returning with Vadius*)

Behold a man who yearns to kiss your hand.
And in presenting him, I have no fear
That he'll profane this cultured atmosphere:
Among our choicest wits, he quite stands out.

PHILAMINTE

Since you present him, his worth's beyond doubt.

TRISSOTIN

In classics, he's the greatest of savants,
And knows more Greek than any man in France.

PHILAMINTE (*to Bélise*)

Greek! Sister, our guest knows Greek! How marvelous!

BÉLISE (*to Armande*)

Greek, Niece! Do you hear?

ARMANDE

Yes, Greek! What joy for *us!*

PHILAMINTE

Think of it! Greek! Oh, Sir, for the love of Greek,
Permit us each to kiss you on the cheek.
      (*Vadius kisses them all save Henriette, who refuses.*)

HENRIETTE

Excusez-moi, monsieur, je n'entends pas le grec.

PHILAMINTE

J'ai pour les livres grecs un merveilleux respect.

VADIUS

Je crains d'être fâcheux[213] par l'ardeur qui m'engage
A vous rendre aujourd'hui, madame, mon hommage,
Et j'aurai pu troubler[214] quelque docte entretien.

PHILAMINTE

Monsieur, avec du grec on ne peut gâter rien.

TRISSOTIN

Au reste, il fait merveille en vers ainsi qu'en prose
Et pourrait, s'il voulait, vous montrer quelque chose.

VADIUS

Le défaut des auteurs dans leurs productions,
C'est d'en tyranniser les conversations;
D'être au palais, au cours, aux ruelles[215], aux tables,
De leur vers fatigants lecteurs infatigables.
Pour moi, je ne vois rien de plus sot, à mon sens,
Qu'un auteur qui partout va gueuser des encens[216];
Qui, des premiers venus saisissant les oreilles,
En fait le plus souvent les martyrs de ses veilles[217].
On ne m'a jamais vu ce fol entêtement,
Et d'un Grec là-dessus je suis le sentiment,
Qui par un dogme exprès défend à tous les sages
L'indigne empressement de lire leurs ouvrages.
Voici de petits vers pour de jeunes amants,
Sur quoi je voudrais bien avoir vos sentiments.

Act III   Scene Three

HENRIETTE

I don't know Greek, Sir; permit me to decline.

PHILAMINTE

I think Greek books are utterly devine.

VADIUS

In my eagerness to meet you, I fear I've come
Intruding on some grave symposium.
Forgive me, Madam, If I've caused confusion.

PHILAMINTE

Ah, Sir, to bring us Greek is no intrusion.

TRISSOTIN

My friend does wonders, too, in verse and prose,
And might well show us something, if he chose.

VADIUS

The fault of authors is their inclination
To dwell upon thier words in conversation,
And whether in parks, or parlors, or at table,
To spout their poems as often as they're able.
How sad to see a writer play the extorter,
Demanding oh's and ah's from every quarter,
And forcing any gathering whatever
To tell him that his labored verse is clever.
I've never embraced the folly of which I speak,
And hold the doctrine of a certain Greek
That men of sense, however well endowed,
Should shun the urge to read their works aloud.
Still, here are some lines, concerning youthful love,
Which I'd be pleased to hear your judgments of.

TRISSOTIN

Vos vers ont des beautés que n'ont point tous les autres.

VADIUS

Les Grâces et Vénus règnent dans tous les vôtres.

TRISSOTIN

Vous avez le tour libre et le beau choix des mots.

VADIUS

On voit partout chez vous l'*ithos* et le *pathos*[218].

TRISSOTIN

Nous avons vu de vous des églogues d'un style
Qui passe en doux attraits Théocrite et Virgile[219].

VADIUS

Vos odes ont un air noble, galant et doux,
Qui laisse de bien loin votre Horace[220] après vous.

TRISSOTIN

Est-il rien d'amoureux comme vos chansonnettes?

VADIUS

Peut-on rien voir d'égal aux sonnets que vous faites?

TRISSOTIN

For verve and beauty, your verses stand alone.

VADIUS

Venus and all the Graces grace your own.

TRISSOTIN

Your choice of words is splendid, and your phrasing.

VADIUS

Your *ethos* and your *pathos* are amazing.

TRISSOTIN

The polished eclogues which you've given us
Surpass both Virgil and Theocritus.

VADIUS

Your odes are noble, gallant, and refined,
And leave your master Horace far behind.

TRISSOTIN

Ah, but your little love songs: what could be sweeter?

VADIUS

As for your well-turned sonnets, none are neater.

TRISSOTIN

Rien qui soit plus charmant que vos petits rondeaux?

VADIUS

Rien de si plein d'esprit que tous vos madrigaux?

TRISSOTIN

Aux ballades surtout vous êtes admirable.

VADIUS

Et dans les bouts-rimés[221] je vous trouve adorable.

TRISSOTIN

Si la France pouvait connaître votre prix...

VADIUS

Si le siècle rendait justice aux beaux esprits...

TRISSOTIN

En carrosse doré vous iriez par les rues.

VADIUS

On verrait le public vous dresser des statues.
    (A Trissotin)
Hom! C'est une ballade, et je veux que tout net
Vous m'en...

TRISSOTIN

Your deft *rondeaux*, are any poems more charming?

VADIUS

Your madrigals—are any more disarming?

TRISSOTIN

Above all, you're a wizard at *ballades*.

VADIUS

At *bouts-rimés*, you always have the odds.

TRISSOTIN

If France would only recognize your merits—

VADIUS

If the age did justice to its finer spirits—

TRISSOTIN

You'd have a gilded coach in which to ride.

VADIUS

Statues of you would rise on every side.
          (*to Trissotin*)
Hem! Now for my *ballade*. Please comment on it
In the frankest—

TRISSOTIN

Avez-vous vu certain petit sonnet
Sur la fièvre qui tient la princesse Uranie?

VADIUS

Oui. Hier il me fut lu dans une compagnie.

TRISSOTIN

Vous en savez l'auteur?

VADIUS

Non; mais je sais fort bien
Qu'à ne le point flatter son sonnet ne vaut rien.

TRISSOTIN

Beaucoup de gens pourtant le trouvent admirable.

VADIUS

Cela n'empêche pas qu'il soit misérable;
Et, si vous l'avez vu, vous serez de mon goût.

TRISSOTIN

Je sais que là-dessus je n'en suis point du tout,
Et que d'un tel sonnet peu de gens sont capables.

VADIUS

Me préserve le ciel d'en faire de semblables!

TRISSOTIN

Have you seen a certain sonnet
About the fever of Princess Uranie?

VADIUS

Yes. It was read to me yesterday, at tea.

TRISSOTIN

Do you know who wrote it?

VADIUS

No, but of this I'm sure:
The sonnet, frankly, is very, very poor.

TRISSOTIN

Oh? Many people have praised it, nonetheless.

VADIUS

That doesn't prevent its being a sorry mess,
And if you've read it, I know you share my view.

TRISSOTIN

Why no, I don't in the least agree with you;
Not many sonnets boast so fine a style.

VADIUS

God grant I never write a thing so vile!

TRISSOTIN

Je soutiens qu'on ne peut en faire de meilleur;
Et ma grande raison, c'est que j'en suis l'auteur.

VADIUS

Vous?

TRISSOTIN

Moi.

VADIUS

Je ne sais donc comment se fit l'affaire.

TRISSOTIN

C'est qu'on fut malheureux de ne pouvoir vous plaire.

VADIUS

Il faut qu'en écoutant j'aie eu l'esprit distrait,
Ou bien que le lecteur m'ait gâté le sonnet.
Mais laissons ce discours, et voyons ma ballade.

TRISSOTIN

La ballade, à mon goût, est une chose fade.
Ce n'en est plus la mode, elle sent son vieux temps.

VADIUS

La ballade pourtant charme beaucoup de gens.

TRISSOTIN

It couldn't be better written, I contend;
And I should know, because I wrote it, friend.

VADIUS

You?

TRISSOTIN

I.

VADIUS

Well, how this happened I can't explain.

TRISSOTIN

What happened was that you found my poem inane.

VADIUS

When I heard the sonnet, I must have been distrait;
Or perhaps 'twas read in an unconvincing way.
But let's forget it; this *ballade* of mine—

TRISSOTIN

Ballades, I think, are rather asinine.
The form's old-hat; it has a musty smell.

VADIUS

Still, many people like it very well.

TRISSOTIN

Cela n'empêche pas qu'elle me déplaise.

VADIUS

Elle n'en reste pas pour cela plus mauvaise.

TRISSOTIN

Elle a pour les pédants de merveilleux appas.

VADIUS

Cependant nous voyons qu'elle ne vous plaît pas.

TRISSOTIN

Vous donnez sottement vos qualités aux autres.

VADIUS

Fort impertinemment vous me jetez les vôtres.

TRISSOTIN

Allez, petit grimaud[222], barbouilleur de papier.

VADIUS

Allez, rimeur de balle[223], opprobre du métier.

TRISSOTIN

Allez, frippier d'écrits[224], imprudent plagiaire.

Act III   Scene Three

TRISSOTIN

That doesn't prevent my finding it dull and flat.

VADIUS

No, but the form is none the worse for that.

TRISSOTIN

The *ballade* is dear to pedants; they adore it.

VADIUS

How curious, then, that you should not be for it.

TRISSOTIN

You see in others your own drab qualities.
(*All rise*)

VADIUS

Don't see your own in me, Sir, if you please.

TRISSOTIN

Be off, you jingling dunce! Let's end this session.

VADIUS

You scribbler! You disgrace to the profession!

TRISSOTIN

You poetaster! You shameless plagiarist!

VADIUS

Allez, cuistre...

PHILAMINTE

Eh! messieurs, que prétendez-vous faire?

TRISSOTIN

Va, va restituer tous les honteux larcins
Que réclament sur toi les Grecs et les Latins.

VADIUS

Va, va t'en faire amende honorable au Parnasse[225]
D'avoir fait à tes vers estropier Horace.

TRISSOTIN

Souviens-toi de ton livre et de son peu de bruit.

VADIUS

Et toi, de ton libraire à l'hopital réduit.

TRISSOTIN

Ma gloire est établie, en vain tu la déchires.

VADIUS

Oui, oui, je te renvoie à l'auteur des *Satires*[226].

TRISSOTIN

Je t'y revoie aussi.

Act III Scene Three

VADIUS

You ink-stained thief!

PHILAMINTE

Oh, gentlemen! Please desist!

TRISSOTIN (*to Vadius*)

Go to the Greeks and Romans, and pay back
The thousand things you've filched from them, you hack.

VADIUS

Go to Parnassus and confess your guilt
For turning Horace into a crazy-quilt.

TRISSOTIN

Think of your book, which caused so little stir.

VADIUS

And you, Sir, think of your bankrupt publisher.

TRISSOTIN

My fame's established; in vain you mock me so.

VADIUS

Do tell. Go look at the *Satires* of Boileau.

TRISSOTIN

Go look at them yourself.

VADIUS

J'ai le contentement
Qu'on voit qu'il m'a traité plus honorablement.
Il me donne en passant une atteinte légère,
Parmi plusieurs auteurs qu'au palais on révère;
Mais jamais dans ses vers il ne te laisse en paix[227],
Et l'on t'y voit partout être en butte à ses traits.

TRISSOTIN

C'est par là que j'y tiens un rang plus honorable.
Il te met dans la foule ainsi qu'un misérable;
Il croit que c'est assez d'un coup pour t'accabler,
Et ne t'a jamais fait l'honneur de redoubler;
Mais il m'attaque à part comme un noble adversaire
Sur qui tout son effort lui semble nécessaire;
Et ses coups, contre moi redoublés en tous lieux,
Montrent qu'il ne se croit à jamais victorieux.

VADIUS

Ma plume t'apprendra quel homme je puis être.

TRISSOTIN

Et la mienne saura te faire voir ton maître.

VADIUS

Je te défie en vers, prose, grec et latin.

TRISSOTIN

Hé bien! nous nous verrons seul à seul chez Barbin[228].

VADIUS

As between us two,
I'm treated there more honorably than you.
He gives me a passing thrust, and links my name
With several authors of no little fame;
But nowhere do his verses leave you in peace;
His witty attacks upon you never cease.

TRISSOTIN

It's therefore I whom he respects the more.
To him, you're one of the crowd, a minor bore;
You're given a single sword-thrust, and are reckoned
Too insignificant to deserve a second.
But me he singles out as a noble foe
Against whom he must strive with blow on blow,
Betraying, by those many strokes, that he
Is never certain of the victory.

VADIUS

My pen will teach you that I'm no poetaster.

TRISSOTIN

And mine will show you, fool, that I'm your master.

VADIUS

I challenge you in verse, prose, Latin and Greek.

TRISSOTIN

We'll meet at Barbin's bookshop, in a week.

Scène IV

TRISSOTIN, PHILAMINTE, ARMANDE, BÉLISE, HENRIETTE

TRISSOTIN

A mon emportement ne donnez aucun blâme:
C'est votre jugement que je défends, madame,
Dans le sonnet qu'il a l'audace d'attaquer.

PHILAMINTE

A vous remettre bien je me veux appliquer.
Mais parlons d'autre affaire. Approchez, Henriette.
Depuis assez longtemps mon âme s'inquiète
De ce qu'aucun esprit en vous ne se fait voir;
Mais je trouve un moyen de vous en faire avoir.

HENRIETTE

C'est prendre un soin pour moi qui n'est pas nécessaire.
Les doctes entretiens ne sont point mon affaire.
J'aime à vivre aisément, et dans tout ce qu'on dit
Il faut se trop peiner pour avoir de l'esprit.
C'est une ambition que je n'ai point en tête.
Je me trouve fort bien, ma mère, d'être bête.
Et j'aime mieux n'avoir que de communs propos
Que de me tourmenter pour dire de beaux mots.

Scene Four

TRISSOTIN, PHILAMINTE, ARMANDE, BÉLISE, HENRIETTE

TRISSOTIN (*to Philaminte*)

Forgive me if my wrath grew uncontrolled;
I felt an obligation to uphold
Your judgment of that sonnet he maligned.

PHILAMINTE

I'll try to mend your quarrel; never mind.
Let's change the subject. Henriette, come here.
I've long been troubled because you don't appear
At all endowed with wit or intellect;
But I've a remedy, now, for that defect.

HENRIETTE

Don't trouble, Mother, I wish no remedy.
Learnèd discourse is not my cup of tea.
I like to take life easy, and I balk
At trying to be a fount of clever talk.
I've no ambition to be a parlor wit,
And if I'm stupid, I don't mind a bit.
I'd rather speak in a plain and common way
Than rack my brains for brilliant things to say.

PHILAMINTE

Oui; mais j'y suis blessée, et ce n'est pas mon compte
De souffrir dans mon sang une pareille honte.
La beauté du visage est un frêle ornement,
Une fleur passagère, un éclat d'un moment,
Et qui n'est attaché qu'à la simple épiderme;
Mais celle de l'esprit est inhérente et ferme.
J'ai donc cherché longtemps un biais de vous donner
La beauté que les ans ne peuvent moissonner,
De faire entrer chez vous le désir des sciences,
De vous insinuer les belles connaissances;
Et la pensée enfin où mes voeux ont souscrit,
C'est d'attacher à vous un homme plein d'esprit,
Et cet homme est monsieur, que je vous détermine[229]
A voir comme l'époux que mon choix vous destine.

HENRIETTE

Moi, ma mère?

PHILAMINTE

Oui, vous. Faites la sotte un peu.

BÉLISE (*à Trissotin)*

Je vous entends. Vos yeux demandent mon aveu
Pour engager ailleurs un coeur que je possède.
Allez, je le veux bien. A ce noeud je vous cède:
C'est un hymen qui fait votre établissement.

Act III Scene Four

PHILAMINTE

I know your shameful tastes, which I decline
To countenance in any child of mine.
Beauty of face is but a transient flower,
A brief adornment, the glory of an hour,
And goes no deeper than the outer skin;
But beauty of mind endures, and lies within.
I've long sought means to cultivate in you
A beauty such as time could not undo,
And plant within your breast a noble yearning
For higher knowledge and the fruits of learning;
And now, at last, I've settled on a plan,
Which is to mate you with a learnèd man—
          (*Gesturing toward Trissotin*)
This gentleman, in short, whom I decree
That you acknowledge as your spouse-to-be.

HENRIETTE

I, Mother?

PHILAMINTE

Yes, you. Stop playing innocent.

BÉLISE (*to Trissotin*)

I understand. Your eyes ask my consent
Before you pledge to her a heart that's mine.
Do so. All claims I willingly resign:
This match will bring you wealth and happiness.

TRISSOTIN (*à Henriette*)

Je ne sais que vous dire en mon ravissement,
Madame, et cet hymen dont je vois qu'on m'honore
Me met...

HENRIETTE

Tout beau[230], monsieur! il n'est pas fait encore;
Ne vous pressez pas tant.

PHILAMINTE

Comme vous répondez!
Savez-vous bien que si...? Suffit, vous m'entendez.
(*à Trissotin*)
Elle se rendra sage. Allons, laissons-la faire.

TRISSOTIN (*to Henriette*)

My rapture, Madam, is more than I can express:
The honor which this marriage will confer
Upon me—

HENRIETTE

Hold! It's not yet settled, Sir;
Don't rush things.

PHILAMINTE

What a reply! How overweening!
Girl, if you dare...Enough, you take my meaning.
(*To Trissotin*)
Just let her be. Her mind will soon be changed.

Scène V

HENRIETTE, ARMANDE

ARMANDE

On voit briller pour vous les soins de notre mère;
Et son choix ne pouvait d'un plus illustre époux ...

HENRIETTE

Si le choix est si beau, que ne le prenez-vous?

ARMANDE

C'est à vous, non à moi, que sa main est donnée.

HENRIETTE

Je vous le cède tout, comme à ma soeur ainée.

ARMANDE

Si l'hymen, comme à vous, me paraissait charmant,
J'accepterais votre offre avec ravissement.

HENRIETTE

Si j'avais, comme vous, les pédants dans la tête,
Je pourrais le trouver un parti fort honnête[231].

Scene Five

HENRIETTE, ARMANDE

ARMANDE

What a brililant match our mother has arranged!
She's found for you a spouse both great and wise.

HENRIETTE

Why don't you take him, if he's such a prize?

ARMANDE

It's you, not I, who are to be his bride.

HENRIETTE

For my elder sister, I'll gladly step aside.

ARMANDE

If I, like you, yearned for the wedded state,
I'd take your offer of so fine a mate.

HENRIETTE

If I, like you, were charmed by pedantry,
I'd think the man a perfect choice for me.

ARMANDE

Cependant, bien qu'ici nos goûts soient différents,
Nous devons obéir, ma soeur, à nos parents;
Une mère a sur nous une entière puissance,
Et vous croyez en vain par votre résistance...

ARMANDE

Our tastes may differ, Sister, but we still
Owe strict obedience to our parents' will;
Whether or not you're fractious and contrary,
You'll wed the man our mother bids you marry...

Scène VI

CHRYSALE, ARISTE, CLITANDRE, HENRIETTE, ARMANDE

CHRYSALE (*à Henriette, en lui présentant Clitandre*)

Allons, ma fille, il faut approuver mon dessein.
Otez ce gant[232]. Touchez à monsieur dans la main,
Et le considérez désormais dans votre âme
En homme dont je veux que vous soyez la femme.

ARMANDE

De ce côté, ma soeur, vos penchants sont fort grands.

HENRIETTE

Il nous faut obéir, ma soeur, à nos parents;
Un père a sur nos voeux une entière puissance.

ARMANDE

Une mère a sa part à notre obéissance

CHRYSALE

Qu'est-ce à dire?

Scene Six

CHRYSALE, ARISTE, CLITANDRE, HENRIETTE, ARMANDE

———————

CHRYSALE (*to Henriette, presenting Clitandre*)

Now, Daughter, you shall do as I command.
Take off that glove, and give this man your hand,
And think of him henceforward as the one
I've chosen as your husband and my son.

ARMANDE

In this case, Sister, you're easy to persuade.

HENRIETTE

Sister, our parents' will must be obeyed;
I'll wed the man my father bids me marry.

ARMANDE

Your mother's blessing, too, is necessary.

CHRYSALE

Just what do you mean?

ARMANDE

Je dis que j'appréhende fort
Qu'ici ma mère et vous ne soyez pas d'accord,
Et c'est un autre époux...

CHRYSALE

Taisez-vous, péronnelle.
Allez philosopher tout le soûl[233] avec elle,
Et de mes actions ne vous mêlez en rien.
Dites-lui ma pensée et l'avertissez bien
Qu'elle ne vienne pas m'échauffer les oreilles.
Allons, vite.

ARISTE

Fort bien: vous faites des merveilles.

CLITANDRE

Quel transport! quelle joie! Ah! que mon sort est doux!

CHRYSALE (à *Clitandre*)

Allons, prenez sa main et passez devant nous.
(à *Ariste*) Menez-la dans sa chambre. Ah! les douces caresses!
Tenez, mon coeur s'émeut à toutes ces tendresses;
Cela regaillardit tout à fait mes vieux jours,
Et je me ressouviens de mes jeunes amours.

ARMANDE

I much regret to state
That Mother has a rival candidate
For the hand of Henri—

CHRYSALE

Hush, you chatterer!
Go prate about philosophy with her,
And cease to meddle in what is my affair.
Tell her it's settled, and bid her to beware
Of angering me by making any fuss.
Go on, now.

ARISTE

Bràvo! This is miraculous.

CLITANDRE

How fortunate I am! What bliss! What joy!

CHRYSALE (*to Clitandre*)

Come, take her hand, now. After you, my boy;
Conduct her to her room. (*To Ariste*) Ah, Brother, this is
A tonic to me; think of those hugs, those kisses!
It warms my old heart, and reminds me of
My youthful days of gallantry and love.

Act IV

Scène I

ARMANDE, PHILAMINTE

ARMANDE

Oui, rien n'a retenu son esprit en balance.
Elle a fait vanité de son obéissance[234].
Son coeur, pour se livrer, à peine devant moi
S'est-il donné le temps d'en recevoir la loi
Et semblait suivre moins les volontés d'un père
Qu'affecter de braver les ordres d'une mère.

PHILAMINTE

Je lui montrerai bien aux lois de qui des deux
Les droits de la raison soumettent tous ses voeux,
Et qui doit gouverner, ou sa mère ou son père,
Ou l'esprit ou le corps, la forme ou la matière[235].

ARMANDE

On vous en devait bien au moins un compliment[236],
Et ce petit monsieur en use étrangement
De vouloir malgré vous devenir votre gendre.

PHILAMINTE

Il n'en est pas encore où son coeur peut prétendre.
Je le trouvais bien fait, et j'aimais vos amours;
Mais, dans ses procédés, il m'a déplu toujours.
Il sait que, Dieu merci, je me mêle d'écrire,
Et jamais il ne m'a prié[237] de lui rien lire.

Scene One

ARMANDE, PHILAMINTE

ARMANDE

Oh, no, she didn't waver or delay,
But, with a flourish, hastened to obey.
Almost before he spoke, she had agreed
To do his bidding, and she appeared, indeed,
Moved by defiance toward her mother, rather
Than deference to the wishes of her father.

PHILAMINTE

I soon shall show her to whose government
The laws of reason oblige her to consent,
And whether it's a matter or form, body or soul,
Father or mother, who is in control.

ARMANDE

The least they could have done was to consult you;
It's graceless of that young man to insult you
By trying to wed your child without your blessing.

PHILAMINTE

He's not yet won. His looks are prepossessing,
And I approved his paying court to you;
But I never liked his manners. He well knew
That writing poetry is a gift of mine,
And yet he never asked to hear a line.

Scène II

CLITANDRE
(*entrant doucement et évitant de se montrer*)
ARMANDE, PHILAMINTE

ARMANDE

Je ne souffrirais point, si j'étais que de vous[238],
Que jamais d'Henriette il pût être l'époux.
On me ferait grand tort d'avoir quelques pensées[239]
Que là-dessus je parle en fille intéressée,
Et que le lâche tour que l'on voit qu'il me fait
Jette au fond de mon coeur quelque dépit secret.
Contre de pareils coups l'âme se fortifie
Du solide secours de la philosophie,
Et par elle on se peut mettre au-dessus de tout;
Mais vous traiter ainsi, c'est vous pousser à bout.
Il est de votre honneur d'être à ses voeux contraire,
Et c'est un homme enfin qui ne doit point vous plaire.
Jamais je n'ai connu, discourant[240] entre nous,
Qu'il eût au fond du coeur de l'estime pour vous.

PHILAMINTE

Petit sot!

ARMANDE

      Quelque bruit que votre gloire fasse,
Toujours à vous louer il a paru de glace.

PHILAMINTE

Le brutal![241]

Scene Two

CLITANDRE
(*entering quietly and listening unseen*)
ARMANDE, PHILAMINTE

———————

ARMANDE

Mother, If I were you, I shouldn't let
That gentleman espouse our Henriette.
Not that I care, of course; I do speak
As someone moved by prejudice or pique,
Or by a heart which, having been forsaken,
Asks vengeance for the wounds which it has taken.
For what I've suffered, philosophy can give
Full consolation, helping one to live
On a high plane, and treat such things with scorn;
But what he's done to you cannot be borne.
Honor requires that you oppose his suit;
Besides, you'd never come to like the brute.
In all our talks, I cannot recollect
His speaking of you with the least respect.

PHILAMINTE

Young whelp!

ARMANDE

        Despite your work's great reputation,
He icily withheld his approbation.

PHILAMINTE

The churl!

ARMANDE

Et vingt fois, comme ouvrages nouveaux,
J'ai lu des vers de vous qu'il n'a point trouvés beaux.

PHILAMINTE

L'impertinent!

ARMANDE

Souvent nous en étions aux prises;
Et vous ne croiriez point combien de sottises...

CLITANDRE

Eh! doucement, de grâce. Un peu de charité,
Madame, ou tout au moins un peu d'honnêteté[242].
Quel mal vous ai-je fais? et quelle est mon offense
Pour armer contre moi toute votre éloquence?
Pour vouloir me détruire et prendre tant de soin
De me rendre odieux aux gens dont j'ai besoin?
Parlez, dites, d'où vient ce courroux effroyable?
Je veux bien que madame en soit juge équitable.

ARMANDE

Si j'avais le courroux dont on veut m'accuser,
Je trouverais assez de quoi l'autoriser[243].
Vous en seriez trop digne, et les premières flammes
S'établissent des droits si sacrés sur les âmes
Qu'il faut perdre fortune et renoncer au jour
Plutôt que de brûler des feux d'un autre amour.
Au changement de voeux nulle horreur ne s'égale,
Et tout coeur infidèle est un monstre en morale.

Act IV Scene Two

ARMANDE

A score of times, I read to him
Your latest poems. He tore them limb from limb.

PHILAMINTE

The beast!

ARMANDE

We quarreled often about your writing.
And you would not believe how harsh, how biting—

CLITANDRE (*to Armande*)

Ah, Madam, a little charity, I pray,
Or a little truthful speaking, anyway.
How have I wronged you? What was the offense
Which makes you seek, by slanderous eloquence,
To rouse against me the distaste and ire
Of those whose good opinion I require?
Speak, Madam, and justify your vicious grudge.
I'll gladly let your mother be our judge.

ARMANDE

Had I the grudge of which I stand accused,
I could defend it, for I've been ill-used.
First love, Sir, is a pure and holy flame
Which makes upon us an eternal claim;
'Twere better to renounce this world, and die,
Than be untrue to such a sacred tie.
Fickleness is a monstrous crime, and in
The moral scale there is no heavier sin.

CLITANDRE

Appelez-vous, madame, une infidélité,
Ce que m'a de votre âme ordonné la fierté?
Je ne fais qu'obéir aux lois qu'elle m'impose,
Et, si je vous offense, elle seule en est la cause.
Vos charmes ont d'abord possédé tout mon coeur.
Il a brûlé deux ans d'une constante ardeur;
Il n'est soins empressés, devoirs, respects, service,
Dont il ne vous ait pas fait d'amoureux sacrifices.
Tous mes feux, tous mes soins, ne peuvent rien sur vous;
Je vous trouve contraire à mes voeux les plus doux:
Ce que vous refusez, je l'offre au choix d'une autre.
Voyez: est-ce madame, ou ma faute ou la vôtre?
Mon coeur court-il au change ou si[244] vous l'y poussez?
Est-ce moi qui vous quitte, ou vous qui me chassez?

ARMANDE

Appelez-vous, monsieur, être à vos voeux contraire
Que de leur arracher ce qu'ils ont de vulgaire
Et vouloir les réduire à cette pureté
Où du parfait amour consiste la beauté?
Vous ne sauriez pour moi tenir votre pensée
Du commerce des sens nette et débarrasser?
Et vous ne goûtez point dans ses plus doux appas
Cette union des coeurs où les corps n'entrent pas?
Vous ne pouvez aimer que d'une amour grossière[245],
Qu'avec tout l'attirail des noeuds de la matière;
Et, pour nourrir les feux que chez nous on produit,
Il faut un mariage, et tout ce qui s'ensuit.
Ah! quel étrange amour! et que les belles âmes
Sont bien loin de brûler de ces terrestres flammes!
Les sens n'ont point de part à toute leurs ardeurs[246],
Et ce beau feu ne veut marier que les coeurs;

CLITANDRE

Do you call it fickleness, *Madame*, to do
What your heart's cold disdain has driven me to?
If, by submitting to its cruel laws,
I've wounded you, your own proud heart's the cause.
My love for you was fervent and entire;
For two whole years it burned with constant fire;
My duty, care, and worship did not falter;
I laid my heart's devotion on your altar.
But all my love and service were in vain;
You dashed the hopes I dared to entertain.
If, thus rejected, I made overtures
To someone else, was that my fault, or yours?
Was I inconsistant, or was I forced to be?
Did I forsake you, or did you banish me?

ARMANDE

Sir, can you say that I've refused your love
When all I sought has been to purge it of
Vulgarity, and teach you that refined
And perfect passion which is of the mind?
Can you not learn an ardor which dispenses
Entirely with the commerce of the senses,
Or see how sweetly spirits may be blended
When bodily desires have been transcended?
Alas, your love is carnal, and cannot rise
Above the plane of gross material ties;
The flame of your devotion can't be fed
Except by marriage, and the marriage bed.
How strange is such a love! Ah oh, how far
Above such earthliness true lovers are!
In their delights, the body plays no part,
And their clear flames but marry heart to heart,

Comme une chose indigne il laisse là le reste.
C'est un feu pur et net comme le feu céleste;
On ne pousse avec lui que d'honnêtes soupirs,
Et l'on ne penche point vers les sales désirs.
Rien d'impur ne se mêle au but qu'on se propose.
On aime pour aimer, et non pour autre chose.
Ce n'est qu'à l'esprit seul que vont tous les transports,
Et l'on ne s'aperçoit jamais qu'on ait un corps.

CLITANDRE

Pour moi, par un malheur, je m'aperçois, madame,
Que j'ai, ne vous déplaise, un corps tout comme une âme;
Je sens qu'il y tient trop pour le laisser à part;
De ces détachements je ne connais point l'art;
Le ciel m'a dénié[247] cette philosophie,
Et mon âme et mon corps marchent de compagnie.
Il n'est rien de plus beau, comme vous avez dit,
Que ces voeux épurés qui ne vont qu'à l'esprit,
Ces unions de coeurs, et ces tendres pensées
Du commerce des sens si bien débarrassées;
Mais ces amours pour moi sont trop subtilisés:
Je suis un peu grossier, comme vous m'accusez;
J'aime avec tout moi-même[248], et l'amour qu'on me donne
En veut, je le confesse, à toute la personne.
Ce n'est pas là matière à de grands châtiments;
Et, sans faire de tort à vos beaux sentiments,
Je vois que dans le monde on suit fort ma méthode,
Et que le mariage est assez à la mode,
Passe pour un lien assez honnête et doux
Pour avoir désiré de me voir votre époux,
Sans que la liberté d'une telle pensée
Ait dû vous donner lieu d'en paraître offensée.

Rejecting all the rest as low and bestial.
Their fire is pure, unsullied, and celestial.
The sighs they breathe are blameless, and express
No filthy hankerings, no fleshliness.
There's no ulterior goal they hunger for.
They love for love's sake, and for nothing more,
And since the spirit is their only care,
Bodies are things of which they're unaware.

CLITANDRE

Well, *I'm* aware, though you may blush to hear it,
That I have both a body and a spirit;
Nor can I part them to my satisfaction;
I fear I lack the power of abstraction
Whereby such philosophic feats are done,
And so my body and soul must live as one.
There's nothing finer, as you say, than these
Entirely spiritual ecstasies,
These marriages of souls, these sentiments
So purified of any taint of sense;
But such love is, for my taste, too ethereal;
I am, as you've complained, a bit material;
I love with all my being, and I confess
That a whole woman is what I would possess.
Need I be damned for feelings of the kind?
With all respect for your high views, I find
That men in general feel my sort of passion,
That marriage still is pretty much in fashion,
And that it's deemed an honorable estate;
So that my asking you to be my mate,
And share with me that good and sweet condition,
Was scarcely an indecent proposition.

ARMANDE

Hé bien, monsieur, hé bien, puisque sans m'écouter,
Vos sentiments brutaux veulent se contenter;
Puisque, pour vous réduire à des ardeurs fidèles,
Il faut des noeuds de chair, des chaînes corporelles,
Si ma mère le veut, je résous mon esprit[249]
A consentir pour vous à ce dont il s'agit.

CLITANDRE

Il n'est plus temps, madame: une autre a pris la place;
Et par un tel retour[250] j'aurai mauvaise grâce
De maltraiter l'asile et blesser les bontés
Où je me suis sauvé de toutes vos fiertés[251].

PHILAMINTE

Mais enfin comptez-vous, monsieur, sur mon suffrage,
Quand vous vous promettez cet autre mariage?
Et, dans vos visions, savez-vous, s'il vous plaît,
Que j'ai pour Henriette un autre époux tout prêt?

CLITANDRE

Eh! madame, voyez votre choix, je vous prie;
Exposez-moi, de grâce, à moins d'ignominie
Et ne me rangez pas à l'indigne destin
De me voir le rival de monsieur Trissotin.
L'amour des beaux esprits, qui chez vous m'est contraire,
Ne pouvait m'opposer un moins noble adversaire.
Il en est, et plusieurs, que pour le bel esprit,
Le mauvais goût du siècle a su mettre en crédit;
Mais monsieur Trissotin n'a pu duper personne
Et chacun rend justice aux écrits qu'il nous donne.

ARMANDE

Ah well, Sir: since you thrust my views aside,
Since your brute instincts must be satisfied,
And since your feelings, to be faithful, must
Be bound by ties of flesh and chains of lust,
I'll force myself, if Mother will consent,
To grant the thing on which you're so intent.

CLITANDRE

It's too late, Madam: another's occupied
Your place; if I now took you as my bride,
I'd wrong a heart which sheltered and consoled me
When, in your pride, you'd treated me so coldly.

PHILAMINTE

Sir, do you dream of my consenting to
This other marriage which you have in view?
Does it not penetrate your mind as yet
That I have other plans for Henriette?

CLITANDRE

Ah, Madam, reconsider, if you please,
And don't expose me thus to mockeries;
Don't put me in the ludicrous position
Of having Trissotin for competition.
What a shabby rival! You couldn't have selected
A wit less honored, a pendant less respected.
We've many pseudo-wits and polished frauds
Whose cleverness the time's bad taste applauds,
But Trissotin fools no one, and indeed
His writings are abhorred by all who read.

LES FEMMES SAVANTES

Hors ceans[252], on le prise en tout lieux ce qu'il vaut;
Et ce qui m'a vingt fois fait tomber de mon haut,
C'est de vous voir au ciel élever des sornettes
Que vous désavoueriez si vous les aviez faites.

PHILAMINTE

Si vous jugez de lui tout autrement que nous,
C'est que nous le voyons par d'autres yeux que vous.

Save in this house, his work is never praised,
And I have been repeatedly amazed
To hear you laud some piece of foolishness
Which, had you written it, you would suppress.

PHILAMINTE

That's how you judge him. We feel otherwise
Because we look at him with different eyes.

Scène III

TRISSOTIN, ARMANDE, PHILAMINTE, CLITANDRE

———————

TRISSOTIN

Je viens vous annoncer une grande nouvelle.
Nous l'avons, en dormant, madame, échappé belle[253]:
Un monde[254] près de nous a passé tout au long,
Est chu tout au travers de notre tourbillon;
Et, s'il eût en chemin rencontré notre terre,
Elle eût été brisée en morceaux comme un verre.

PHILAMINTE

Remettons ce discours pour une autre saison,
Monsieur n'y trouverait ni rime ni raison;
Il fait profession de chérir l'ignorance,
Et de haïr surtout l'esprit et la science.

CLITANDRE

Cette vérité veut quelque adoucissement.
Je m'explique, madame; et je hais seulement
La science et l'esprit qui gâtent les personnes.
Ce sont choses de soi qui sont belles et bonnes;
Mais j'aimerais mieux être au rang des ignorants
Que de me voir savant comme certaines gens.

Scene Three

TRISSOTIN, ARMANDE, PHILAMINTE, CLITANDRE

TRISSOTIN (*to Philaminte*)

I bring you, Madam, some startling news I've heard.
Last night, a near-catastrophe occurred:
While we were all asleep, a comet crossed
Our vortex, and the Earth was all but lost;
Had it collided with our world, alas,
We'd have been shattered into bits, like glass.

PHILAMINTE

Let's leave that subject for another time;
This gentleman, I fear, would see no rhyme
Or reason in it; it's ignorance he prizes;
Learning and wit are things which he despises.

CLITANDRE

Kindly permit me, Madam, to restate
Your summary of my views: I only hate
Such wit and learning as twist men's brains awry.
Those things are excellent in themselves, but I
Had rather be an ignorant man, by far,
Than learnèd in the way some people are.

TRISSOTIN

Pour moi, je ne tiens pas, quelque effet qu'on suppose,
Que la science soit pour[255] gâter quelque chose.

CLITANDRE

Et c'est mon sentiment qu'en faits comme en propos
La science est sujette à faire de grands sots.

TRISSOTIN

Le paradoxe est fort.

CLITANDRE

      Sans être fort habile,
La preuve m'en serait, je pense, assez facile.
Si les raisons manquaient, je suis sûr qu'en tout cas
Les exemples fameux ne me manqueraient pas.

TRISSOTIN

Vous en pourriez citer qui ne concluraient guère.

CLITANDRE

Je n'irais pas bien loin pour trouver mon affaire.

TRISSOTIN

Pour moi, je ne vois pas ces exemples fameux.

CLITANDRE

Moi, je les vois si bien qu'ils me crèvent les yeux.

TRISSOTIN

Well, as for me, I hold that learning never
Could twist a man in any way whatever.

CLITANDRE

And I assert that learning often breeds
Men who are foolish both in words and deed.

TRISSOTIN

What a striking paradox!

CLITANDRE

Though I'm no wit,
I'd have no trouble, I think, in proving it.
If arguments should fail, I'm sure I'd find
That living proofs came readily to mind.

TRISSOTIN

The living proofs you gave might not persuade.

CLITANDRE

I'd not look far before my point was made.

TRISSOTIN

I cannot think, myself, of such a case.

CLITANDRE

I can; indeed, it stares me in the face.

TRISSOTIN

J'ai cru jusques ici que c'était l'ignorance
Qui faisait les grands sots, et non pas la science.

CLITANDRE

Vous avez cru fort mal, et je vous suis garant
Qu'un sot savant est sot plus qu'un sot ignorant.

TRISSOTIN

Le sentiment commun est contre vos maximes[256],
Puisque ignorant et sot sont termes synonymes.

CLITANDRE

Si vous le voulez prendre aux usages du mot,
L'alliance est plus grande entre pédant et sot.

TRISSOTIN

La sottise dans l'un se fait voir toute pure.

CLITANDRE

Et l'étude dans l'autre ajoute à la nature.

TRISSOTIN

Le savoir garde en soi son mérite éminent.

CLITANDRE

Le savoir dans un fat devient impertinent[257].

TRISSOTIN

I thought it was by ignorance, and not
By learning, Sir, that great fools were begot.

CLITANDRE

Well, you thought wrongly. It's a well-known rule
That no fool's greater than a learnèd fool.

TRISSOTIN

Our common usage contradicts that claim,
Since "fool" and "ignoramus" mean the same.

CLITANDRE

You think those words synonymous! Oh no, Sir!
You'll find that "fool" and "pendant" are much closer.

TRISSOTIN

"Fool" denotes plain and simple foolishness.

CLITANDRE

"Pendant" denotes the same, in fancy dress.

TRISSOTIN

The quest for knowledge is noble and august.

CLITANDRE

But knowledge, in a pedant, turns to dust.

TRISSOTIN

Il faut que l'ignorance ait pour vous de grands charmes,
Puisque pour elle ainsi vous prenez tant les armes.

CLITANDRE

Si pour moi l'ignorance a des charmes bien grands,
C'est depuis qu'à mes yeux s'offrent certains savants.

TRISSOTIN

Ces certains savants-là peuvent, à les connaître,
Valoir certaines gens que nous voyons paraître.

CLITANDRE

Oui, si l'on s'en rapporte à ces certains savants;
Mais on n'en convient pas chez ces certaines gens.

PHILAMINTE (*à Clitandre*)

Il me semble, monsieur....

CLITANDRE

    Eh! madame, de grâce,
Monsieur est assez fort sans qu'à son aide on passe:
Je n'ai déjà que trop d'un si rude assaillant[258];
Et si je me défends, ce n'est qu'en reculant.

ARMANDE

Mais, l'offensante aigreur de chaque repartie
Dont vous ...

TRISSOTIN

It's clear that ignorance has great charms for you,
Or else you wouldn't defend it as you do.

CLITANDRE

I came to see the charms of ignorance when
I made the acquaintance of certain learnèd men.

TRISSOTIN

Those certain learnèd men, it may turn out,
Are better than certain folk who strut about.

CLITANDRE

The learnèd men would say so, certainly;
But then, those certain folk might not agree.

PHILAMINTE (*to Clitandre*)

I think, Sir—

CLITANDRE

    Madam, spare me, please. This rough
Assailant is already fierce enough.
Don't join him, pray, in giving me a beating.
I shall preserve myself, now, by retreating.

ARMANDE

You, with your brutal taunts, were the offender;
'Twas you—

CLITANDRE

Autre second[259], je quitte la partie.

PHILAMINTE

On souffre aux entretiens ces sortes de combats,
Pourvu qu'à la personne on ne s'attaque pas.

CLITANDRE

Eh! mon Dieu, tout cela n'a rien dont il s'offense;
Il entend raillerie[260] autant qu'homme de France,
Et de bien d'autres traits il s'est senti piquer
Sans que jamais sa gloire[261] ait fait que s'en moquer.

TRISSOTIN

Je ne m'étonne pas, au combat que j'essuie[262],
De voir prendre à monsieur la thèse qu'il appuie.
Il est fort enfoncé dans la cour, c'est tout dit[263]:
La cour, comme on le sait, ne tient pas pour l'esprit;
Elle a quelque intérêt d'appuyer l'ignorance,
Et c'est en courtisan qu'il en prend la défense.

CLITANDRE

Vous en voulez beaucoup[264] à cette pauvre cour,
Et son malheur est grand de voir que chaque jour
Vous autres, beaux esprits, vous réclamiez contre elle,
Que de tous vos chagrins vous lui fassiez querelle,
Et, sur son méchant goût lui faisant son procès
N'accusiez que lui seul de vos méchants succès[265].
Permettez-moi, monsieur Trissotin, de vous dire,
Avec tout le respect que votre nom m'inspire,
Que vous feriez fort bien, vos confrères et vous,
De parler de la cour d'un ton un peu plus doux;

CLITANDRE

More reinforcements! I surrender.

PHILAMINTE

Sir, witty repartee is quite all right,
But personal attacks are impolite.

CLITANDRE

Good Lord, he's quite unhurt, as one can tell.
No one in France takes ridicule so well.
For years he's heard men gibe at him, and scoff,
And in his smugness merely laughed it off.

TRISSOTIN

I'm not surprised to hear this gentleman say
The things he's said in this unpleasant fray.
He's much at court, and as one might expect,
He shares the court's mistrust of intellect,
And, as a courtier, defends with zest
The ignorance that's in its interest.

CLITANDRE

You're very hard indeed on the poor court,
Which hears each day how people of your sort,
Who deal in intellectual ware, decry it,
Complain that their careers are blighted by it,
Deplore its wretched taste, and blame their own
Unhappy failures on that cause alone.
Permit me, Mister Trissotin, with due
Respect for your great name, to say that you
And all your kind would do well to discuss
The court in tones less harsh and querulous;

Qu'à le bien prendre, au fond, elle n'est pas si bête
Que vous autres, messieurs, vous vous mettez en tête;
Qu'elle a du sens commun pour se connaître à tout[266],
Que chez elle on se peut former quelque bon goût,
Et que l'esprit du monde y vaut, sans flatterie,
Tout le savoir obscur de la pédanterie.

TRISSOTIN

De son bon goût, monsieur, nous voyons des effets.

CLITANDRE

Où voyez-vous, monsieur, qu'elle l'ait si mauvais?

TRISSOTIN

Ce que je vois, monsieur, c'est que pour la science
Rasius et Baldus[267] font honneur à la France,
Et que tout leur mérite, exposé fort au jour,
N'attire point les yeux et les dons de la cour.

CLITANDRE

Je vois votre chagrin, et que par modestie
Vous ne vous mettez point, monsieur, de la partie;
Et, pour ne vous point mettre aussi dans le propos,
Que font-ils pour l'Etat vos habiles héros?
Qu'est-ce que leurs écrits lui rendent de service,
Pour accuser la cour d'une horrible injustice
Et se plaindre en tous lieux que leurs doctes noms
Elle manque à verser la faveur de ses dons?
Leur savoir à la France est beaucoup nécessaire!
Et des livres qu'ils font la cour a bien affaire!
Il semble à trois gredins[268], dans leur petit cerveau,
Que, pour être imprimés[269] et relié en veau,

That the court is not so short of wit and brain
As you and all your scribbling friends maintain;
That all things, there, are viewed with common sense,
That good taste, too, is much in evidence,
And that its knowledge of the world surpasses
The fusty learnings of pedantic asses.

TRISSOTIN

It has good taste, you say? If only it had!

CLITANDRE

What makes you say, Sir, that its taste is bad?

TRISSOTIN

What makes me say so? Rasiùs and Baldùs
Do France great honor by what their pens produce,
Yet the court pays these scholars no attention,
And neither of them has received a pension.

CLITANDRE

I now perceive your grievance, and I see
That you've left your own name out, from modesty.
Well, let's not drag it into our debate.
Just tell me: how have your heroes served the State?
What are their writings worth, that they expect
Rewards, and charge the nation with neglect?
Why should they whine, these learnèd frineds of yours,
At not receiving gifts and sinecures?
A precious lot they've done for France, indeed!
Their times are just what court and country need!
The vanity of such beggars makes me laugh:
Because they're set in type and bound in calf,

Les voilà dans l'Etat d'importantes personnes;
Qu'avec leur plume ils font les destins des couronnes;
Qu'au moindre petit bruit de leurs productions
Ils doivent voir chez eux voler les pensions;
Que sur eux l'univers a la vue attachée;
Que partout de leur nom la gloire est épanchée,
Et qu'en science ils sont des prodiges fameux,
Pour savoir ce qu'on dit les autres avant eux,
Pour avoir eu trente ans des yeux et des oreilles,
Pour avoir employé neuf ou dix mille veilles
A se bien barbouiller de grec et de latin,
Et se charger l'esprit d'un ténébreux butin
De tous les vieux fatras qui traînent dans les livres;
Gens qui de leur savoir paraissent toujours ivres;
Riches, pour tout mérite, en babil importun,
Inhabiles à tout, vides de sens commun,
Et pleins d'un ridicule et d'une impertinence[270]
A décrier partout l'esprit et la science.

PHILAMINTE

Votre chaleur est grande, et cet emportement
De la nature en vous marque le mouvement;
C'est le nom de rival qui dans votre âme excite...

236

They think that they're illustrious citizens;
That the fate of nations hang upon their pens;
That the least mention of their work should bring
The pensions flocking in on eager wing;
That the whole universe, with one wide stare,
Admire them; that their fame is everywhere,
And that they're wondrous wise because they know
What others said before them, long ago—
Because they've given thirty years of toil
And eyestrain to acquire, by midnight oil,
Some jumbled Latin and some garbled Greek,
And overload their brains with the antique
Obscurities which lie about in books.
These bookworms, with their smug, myopic looks,
Are full of pompous talk and windy unction;
They have no common sense, no useful function,
And could, in short, persuade the human race
To think all wit and learning a disgrace.

PHILAMINTE

You speak most heatedly, and it is clear
What feelings prompt you to be so severe;
Your rival's presence, which seems to irk you greatly—

Scène IV

JULIEN, TRISSOTIN, PHILAMINTE, CLITANDRE, ARMANDE

———————

JULIEN

Le savant qui tantôt vous a rendu visite,
Et de qui j'ai l'honneur de me voir le valet,
Madame, vous exhorte à lire ce billet.

PHILAMINTE

Quelque important que soit ce qu'on veut que je lise,
Apprenez, mon ami, que c'est une sottise
De se venir jeter au travers d'un discours,
Et qu'aux gens[271] d'un logis il faut avoir recours,
Afin de s'introduire en valet qui sait vivre.

JULIEN

Je noterai cela, madame, dans mon livre.

PHILAMINTE *(lit)*

"Trissotin s'est vanté, madame, qu'il épouserait votre
fille. Je vous donne avis que sa philosophie n'en veut qu'à
vos richesses, et que vous ferez bien de ne point conclure
ce mariage que vous n'ayez vu le poème que je compose
contre lui. En attendant cette peinture, où je prétends vous
le dépeindre de toutes ses couleurs, je vous envoie
Horace, Virgile, Térence et Catulle[272], où vous verrez
notés en marge tous les endroits qu'il a pillés."

Scene Four

JULIEN, TRISSOTIN, PHILAMINTE, CLITANDRE, ARMANDE

JULIEN

That learnèd man who visited you lately,
And whose valet I have the honor to be,
Sends you this note, *Madame*, by way of me.

PHILAMINTE

Whatever the import of this note you bring,
Do learn, my friend, that it's a graceless thing
To interrupt a conversation so,
And that a rightly trained valet would go
To the servants first, and ask them for admission.

JULIEN

Madam, I'll bear in mind your admonition.

PHILAMINTE (*reading*)

"Trissotin boasts, Madam, that he is going to marry your
daughter. Let me warn you that that great thinker is thinking
only of your wealth, and that you would do well to put off
the marriage until you have seen the poem which I am now
composing against him. It is to be a portrait in verse, and I
propose to depict him for you in his true colors. Meanwhile,
I am sending herewith the works of Horace, Virgil, Terence,
And Catullus, in the margins of which I have marked, for
your benefit, all the passages which he has plundered."

PHILAMINTE (*poursuit*)

Voilà, sur cet hymen que je me suis promis,
Un mérite attaqué de beaucoup d'ennemis;
Et ce déchaînement aujourd'hui me convie
A faire une action qui confonde l'envie,
Qui lui fasse sentir que l'effort qu'elle fait
De ce qu'elle veut rompre aura pressé l'effet[273].
Reportez tout cela sur l'heure à votre maître,
Et lui dites[274] qu'afin de lui faire connaître
Quel grand état je fais de ses nobles avis,
Et comme je les crois dignes d'être suivis,
Dès ce soir à monsieur je marierai ma fille.
Vous, monsieur, comme ami de toute la famille,
A signer leur contrat vous pourrez assister[275],
Et je vous y veux bien de ma part inviter.
Armande, prenez soin d'envoyer au notaire[276]
Et d'aller avertir votre soeur de l'affaire.

ARMANDE

Pour avertir ma soeur, il n'en est pas besoin,
Et monsieur que voilà saura prendre le soin
De courir lui porter bientôt cette nouvelle
Et diposer son coeur à vous être rebelle.

PHILAMINTE

Nous verrons qui sur elle aura plus de pouvoir,
Et si je la saurai réduire à son devoir.
  (*Elle s'en va*)

PHILAMINTE (*reading*)

Well, well! To thwart that match which I desire,
A troop of enemies has opened fire
Upon this worthy man; but I'll requite
By one swift action their dishonest spite,
And show them all that their combined assault
Has only hastened what they strove to halt.
(*to Julien*)
Take back those volumes to your master, and
Inform him, so that he'll clearly understand
Precisely how much value I have set
Upon his sage advice, that Henriette
(*Pointing to Trissotin*)
Shall wed this gentleman, this very night.
(*To Clitandre*)
Sir, you're a friend of the family. I invite
You most sincerely to remain and see
The contract signed, as shortly it shall be.
Armande, you'll send for the notary, and prepare
Your sister for her part in this affair.

ARMANDE

No need for me to let my sister know;
This gentleman, I'm sure, will quickly go
To tell her all the news, and seek as well
To prompt her saucy spirit to rebel.

PHILAMINTE

We'll see by whom her spirit will be swayed;
It doesn't suit me to be disobeyed.

LES FEMMES SAVANTES

ARMANDE

J'ai grand regret, monsieur, de voir qu'à vos visées[277]
Les choses ne soient pas tout à fait disposées.

CLITANDRE

Je m'en vais travailler, madame, avec ardeur,
A ne vous point laisser ce grand regret au coeur.

ARMANDE

J'ai peur que votre effort n'ait pas trop bonne issue.

CLITANDRE

Peut-être verrez-vous votre crainte déçue.

ARMANDE

Je le souhaite ainsi.

CLITANDRE

J'en suis persuadé,
Et que de votre appui je serai secondé.

ARMANDE

Oui, je vais vous servir de toute ma puissance.

CLITANDRE

Et ce service est sûr de ma reconnaissance.

ARMANDE

I'm very sorry for you, Sir; it seems
things haven't gone according to your schemes.

CLITANDRE

Madam, I mean to do my very best
To lift that weight of sorrow from your breast.

ARMANDE

I fear, Sir, that your hopes are not well-grounded.

CLITANDRE

It may be that your fear will prove ill-founded.

ARMANDE

I hope so.

CLITANDRE

I believe you; nor do I doubt
That you'll do all you can to help me out.

ARMANDE

To serve your cause shall be my sole endeavor.

CLITANDRE

For that, you'll have my gratitude forever.

Scène V

CHRYSALE, ARISTE, HENRIETTE, CLITANDRE

———————

CLITANDRE

Sans votre appui, monsieur, je serai malheureux:
Madame votre femme a rejeté mes voeux,
Et son coeur prévenu veut Trissotin pour gendre.

CHRYSALE

Mais quelle fantaisie a-t-elle donc pu prendre?
Pourquoi diantre vouloir ce monsieur Trissotin?

ARISTE

C'est par l'honneur qu'il a de rimer à latin[278]
Qu'il a sur son rival emporté l'avantage.

CLITANDRE

Elle veut dès ce soir faire ce mariage.

CHRYSALE

Dès ce soir?

CLITANDRE

Dès ce soir.

Scene Five

CHRYSALE, ARISTE, HENRIETTE, CLITANDRE

CLITANDRE

I shall be lost unless you help me, Sir;
Your wife's rejected my appeals to her,
And chosen Trissotin for her son-in-law.

CHRYSALE

Damn it, what ails the woman? I never saw
What in this Trissotin could attract her.

ARISTE

He versifies in Latin, and that's a factor
Which makes him, in her view, the better man.

CLITANDRE

To marry them tonight, Sir, is her plan.

CHRYSALE

Tonight?

CLITANDRE

Tonight.

CHRYSALE

Et dès ce soir je veux,
Pour la contrecarrer, vous marier tous deux.

CLITANDRE

Pour dresser le contrat, elle envoie au notaire.

CHRYSALE

Et je vais le quérir pour celui qu'il doit faire.

CLITANDRE

Et madame doit être instruite par sa soeur
De l'hymen où l'on veut qu'elle apprête son coeur.

CHRYSALE

Et moi je lui commande, avec pleine puissance,
De préparer sa main à cette autre alliance.
Ah! je leur ferai voir si, pour donner la loi,
Il est dans ma maison d'autre maître que moi.
Nous allons revenir, songez à nous attendre.
Allons, suivez mes pas, mon frère, et vous, mon gendre.

HENRIETTE (*à Ariste*)

Hélas! dans cette humeur conservez-le toujours.

ARISTE

J'emploierai toute chose à servir vos amours.

Act IV Scene Five

CHRYSALE

Her plan, then, will miscarry.
I promise that, tonight, you two shall marry.

CLITANDRE

She's having a contract drawn by the notary.

CHRYSALE

Well, he shall draw another for me.

CLITANDRE (*indicating Henriette*)

Armande has orders to inform this lady
Of the wedding match for which she's to be ready.

CHRYSALE

And I inform her that, by my command,
It's you on whom she shall bestow her hand.
This is my house, and I shall make it clear
That I'm the one and only master here.
    (*To Henriette*)
Wait, Daughter; we'll join you when our errand's done.
Come, Brother, follow me; you too, my son.

HENRIETTE (*to Ariste*)

Please keep him in this mood, whatever you do.

ARISTE

I'll do my utmost for your love and you.

CLITANDRE

Quelque secours puissant qu'on promette à ma flamme,
Mon plus solide espoir, c'est votre coeur, madame.

HENRIETTE

Pour mon coeur, vous pouvez vous assurer de lui.

CLITANDRE

Je ne puis qu'être heureux quand j'aurai son appui[279].

HENRIETTE

Vous voyez à quels noeuds on prétend le contraindre.

CLITANDRE

Tant qu'il sera pour moi, je ne vois rien à craindre.

HENRIETTE

Je vais tout essayer pour nos voeux les plus doux;
Et, si tous mes efforts ne me donnent à vous
Il est une retraite[280] où notre âme se donne,
Qui m'empêchera d'être à toute autre pesonne.

CLITANDRE

Veuille le juste ciel me garder en ce jour
De recevoir de vous cette preuve d'amour.

CLITANDRE

Whatever aid our kind allies may lend,
It's your true heart on which my hopes depend.

HENRIETTE

As to my heart, of that you may be sure.

CLITANDRE

If so, my own is happy and secure.

HENRIETTE

I must be strong, so as not to be coerced.

CLITANDRE

Cling to our love, and let them do their worst.

HENRIETTE

I'll do my best to make our cause prevail;
But if my hope of being yours should fail,
And if it seems I'm to be forced to marry,
A convent cell shall be my sanctuary.

CLITANDRE

Heaven grant that you need never give to me
Such painful proof of your fidelity.

Act V

Scène I

HENRIETTE, TRISSOTIN

———————

HENRIETTE

C'est sur le mariage où[281] ma mère s'apprête
Que j'ai voulu, monsieur, vous parler tête à tête,
Et j'ai cru, dans le trouble où je vois la maison
Que je pourrais vous faire écouter la raison.
Je sais qu'avec mes voeux vous me jugez capable
De vous porter en dot un bien[282] considérable;
Mais l'argent, dont on voit tant de gens faire cas,
Pour un vrai philosophe a d'indignes appas,
Et le mépris du bien et des grandeurs frivoles
Ne doit point éclater dans vos seules paroles.

TRISSOTIN

Aussi n'est-ce point là ce qui me charme en vous;
Et vos brillants attraits, vos yeux perçants et doux,
Votre grâce et votre air, sont les biens, les richesses,
Qui vous ont attiré mes voeux et mes tendresses;
C'est de ces seuls trésors que je suis amoureux.

HENRIETTE

Je suis fort bien redevable à vos feux généreux.
Cet obligeant amour a de quoi me confondre,
Et j'ai regret, monsieur, de n'y pouvoir répondre.
Je vous estime autant qu'on saurait estimer,
Mais je trouve un obstacle à vous pouvoir aimer.

Scene One

HENRIETTE, TRISSOTIN

———————————

HENRIETTE

It seems to me that we two should confer
About this contemplated marriage, Sir,
Since it's reduced our household to dissension.
Do give my arguments your kind attention.
I know that you expect to realize,
By wedding me, a dowry of some size;
Yet money, which so many men pursue,
should bore a true philosopher like you,
And your contempt for riches should be shown
In your behavior, not in words alone.

TRISSOTIN

It's not in wealth that your attraction lies:
Your sparkling charms, your soft yet flashing eyes,
Your airs, your graces—it is these in which
My ravished heart perceives you to be rich,
These treasures only which I would possess.

HENRIETTE

I'm honored by the love which you profess,
Although I can't see what I've done to earn it,
And much regret, Sir, that I can't return it.
I have the highest estimation of you,
But there's one reason why I cannot love you.

Un coeur, vous le savez, à deux ne saurait être,
Et je sens que du mien Clitandre s'est fait maître.
Je sais qu'il a bien moins de mérite que vous,
Que j'ai de méchants yeux pour le choix d'un époux,
Que par cent beaux talents vous devriez me plaire;
Je vois bien que j'ai tort, mais je n'y puis que faire[283],
Et tout ce que sur moi peut le raisonnement,
C'est de me vouloir mal[284] d'un tel aveuglement.

TRISSOTIN

Le don de votre main, où l'on me fait prétendre,
Me livrera ce coeur que possède Clitandre,
Et par mille doux soins j'ai lieu de présumer
Que je pourrai trouver l'art de me faire aimer.

HENRIETTE

Non; à ses premiers voeux[285] mon âme est attachée,
Et ne peut de vos soins, monsieur, être touchée.
Avec vous librement j'ose ici m'expliquer,
Et mon aveu n'a rien qui vous doive choquer.
Cette amoureuse ardeur qui dans les coeurs s'excite
N'est point, comme l'on sait, un effet du mérite;
Le caprice y prend part, et quand quelqu'un nous plaît,
Souvent nous avons peine à dire pourquoi c'est.
Si l'on aimait, monsieur, par choix et par sagesse,
Vous auriez tout mon coeur et toute ma tendresse;
Mais l'on voit que l'amour se gouverne autrement.
Laissez-moi, je vous prie, à mon aveuglement,
Et ne vous servez point de cette violence
Que pour vous on veut faire à mon obéissance.
Quand on est honnête homme[286], on ne veut rien devoir
A ce que des parents ont sur nous de pouvoir.
On répugne à se faire immoler ce qu'on aime,
Et l'on veut n'obtenir un coeur que de lui-même.

A heart's devotion cannot be divided,
And it's Clitandre on whom my heart's decided.
I know he lacks your merits, which are great,
That I'm obtuse to choose him for my mate,
That you should please me by your gifts and wit;
I know I'm wrong, but there's no help for it;
Though reason chides me for my want of sense,
My heart clings blindly to its preference.

TRISSOTIN

When I am given your hand and marriage vow,
I'll claim the heart Clitandre possesses now,
And I dare hope that I can then incline
That heart, by sweet persuasions, to be mine.

HENRIETTE

No, no: first love, Sir, is too strong a feeling.
All your persuasions could not prove appealing.
Let me, upon this point, be blunt and plain,
Since nothing I shall say could cause you pain.
The fires of love, which set our hearts aglow,
Aren't kindled by men's merits, as you know.
They're most capricious; when someone takes our eye,
We're often quite unable to say why.
If, Sir, our loves were based on wise selection,
You would have all my heart, all my affection;
But love quite clearly doesn't work that way.
Indulge me in my blindness, then, I pray,
And do not show me, sir, so little mercy
As to desire that others should coerce me.
What man of honor would care to profit by
A parent's power to make a child comply?
To win a lady's hand by such compulsion,
And not by love, would fill him with revulsion.

Ne poussez point ma mère à vouloir, par son choix,
Exercer sur mes voeux la rigueur de ses droits.
Otez-moi votre amour, et portez à quelque autre
Les hommages d'un coeur aussi cher[287] que le vôtre.

TRISSOTIN

Le moyen que ce coeur puisse vous contenter?
Imposez-lui des lois qu'il puisse exécuter.
De ne vous point aimer peut-il être capable?
A moins que vous cessiez, madame, d'être aimable[288],
Et d'étaler aux yeux les célestes appas...?

HENRIETTE

Eh! monsieur, laissons là ce galimatias[289].
Vous avez tant d'Iris, de Philis, d'Amarantes[290],
Que partout dans vos vers vous peignez si charmantes,
Et pour qui vous jurez tant d'amoureuse ardeur...

TRISSOTIN

C'est mon esprit qui parle, et ce n'est pas mon coeur.
D'elles on ne me voit amoureux qu'en poète;
Mais j'aime tout de bon l'adorable Henriette.

HENRIETTE

Eh! de grâce, monsieur ...

TRISSOTIN

Si c'est vous offenser,
Mon offense envers vous n'est pas prête à cesser.
Cette ardeur, jusqu'ici de vos yeux ignorée,
Vous consacre des voeux d'éternelle durée;

Don't then, I beg you, urge my mother to make
Me bow to her authority for your sake.
Take back the love you offer, and reserve it
For some fine woman who will more deserve it.

TRISSOTIN

Alas, what you command I cannot do.
I'm powerless to retract my love for you.
How shall I cease to worship you, unless
You cease to dazzle me with loveliness,
To stun my heart with beauty, to enthrall—

HENRIETTE

Oh, come, Sir; no more nonsense. You have all
These Irises and Phyllises whose great
Attractiveness your verses celebrate,
And whom you so adore with so much art—

TRISSOTIN

My mind speaks in those verses, not my heart.
I love those ladies in my poems merely,
While Henriette, alone, I love sincerely.

HENRIETTE

Please, Sir—

TRISSOTIN

          If by so speaking I offend,
I fear that my offense will never end.
My ardor, which I've hidden hitherto,
Belongs for all eternity to you;

Rien n'en peut arrêter les aimables transports;
Et, bien que vos beautés condamnent mes efforts,
Je ne puis refuser le secours d'une mère
Qui prétend couronner une flamme si chère,
Et, pourvu que j'obtienne un bonheur si charmant[291],
Pourvu que je vous aie, il n'importe comment.

HENRIETTE

Mais savez-vous qu'on risque un peu plus qu'on ne pense
A vouloir sur un coeur user de violence;
Qu'il ne fait pas bien sûr, à vous le trancher net[292],
D'épouser une fille en dépit qu'elle en ait[293],
Et qu'elle peut aller, en se voyant contraindre,
A des ressentiments que le mari doit craindre?

TRISSOTIN

Un tel discours n'a rien dont je sois altéré[294]:
A tous évènements le sage est préparé.
Guéri par la raison des faiblesses vulgaires,
Il se met au-dessus de ces sortes d'affaires,
Et n'a garde de prendre aucune ombre d'ennui
De tout ce qui n'est pas pour[295] dépendre de lui.

HENRIETTE

En vérité, monsieur, je suis de vous ravie;
Et je ne pensais pas que la philosophie
Fût si belle qu'elle est, d'instruire ainsi les gens
A porter constamment[296] de pareils accidents.
Cette fermeté d'âme à vous si singulière[297]
Mérite qu'on lui donne une illustre matière,
Est digne de trouver qui prenne[298] avec amour
Les soins continuels de la mettre en son jour;
Et comme, à dire vrai, je n'oserai me croire
Bien propre à lui donner tout l'éclat de sa gloire[299],

Act V Scene One

I'll love you till this beating heart has stopped;
And, though you scorn the tactics I adopt,
I can't refuse your mother's aid in gaining
The joy I'm so desirous of obtaining.
If the sweet prize I long for can be won,
And you be mine, I care not how it's done.

HENRIETTE

But don't you see that it's a risky course
To take possession of a heart by force;
That things, quite frankly, can go very ill
When a woman's made to wed against her will,
And that, in her resentment, she won't lack
For means to vex her spouse, and pay him back?

TRISSOTIN

I've no anxiety about such things.
The wise man takes whatever fortune brings.
Transcending vulgar weaknesses, his mind
Looks down unmoved on mishaps of the kind,
Nor does he feel the least distress of soul
Regarding matters not in his control.

HENRIETTE

You fascinate me, Sir; I'm much impressed.
I didn't know philosophy possessed
Such powers, and could teach men to endure
Such tricks of fate without discomfiture.
Your lofty patience ought, Sir, to be tested,
So that its greatness could be manifested;
It calls, Sir, for a wife who'd take delight
In making you display it, day and night;
But since I'm ill-equipped, by temperment,
To prove your virtue to its full extent,

Je le laisse à quelque autre et vous jure entre nous
Que je renonce au bien[300] de vous voir mon époux.

TRISSOTIN

Nous allons voir bientôt comment ira l'affaire,
Et l'on a là-dedans fait venir le notaire.

I'll leave that joy to one more qualified,
And let some other woman be your bride.

TRISSOTIN

Well, we shall see. The notary for whom
Your mother sent is in the neighboring room.

Scène II

CHRYSALE, CLITANDRE, MARTINE, HENRIETTE

_____

CHRYSALE

Ah! ma fille, je suis bien aise de vous voir.
Allons, venez-vous-en faire votre devoir
Et soumettre vos voeux aux volontés d'un père.
Je veux, je veux apprendre à vivre[301] à votre mère;
Et, pour le mieux braver, voilà, malgré ses dents[302],
Martine que j'amène et rétablis céans.

HENRIETTE

Vos résolutions sont dignes de louange.
Gardez que cette humeur, mon père, ne vous change.
Soyez ferme à vouloir ce que vous souhaitez,
Et ne vous laissez point séduire à vos bontés[303].
Ne vous relâchez pas, et faites bien en sorte
D'empêcher que sur vous ma mère ne l'emporte[304].

CHRYSALE

Comment! Me prenez-vous ici pour un benêt?

HENRIETTE

M'en préserve le ciel!

Scene Two

CHRYSALE, CLITANDRE, MARTINE, HENRIETTE

CHRYSALE

Ah, Daughter, I'm pleased indeed to find you here.
Prepare to show obedience, now, my dear,
By doing as your father bids you do.
I'm going to teach your mother a thing or two;
And, first of all, as you can see, I mean
To thwart her will and reinstate Martine.

HENRIETTE

I much admire the stands which you have taken.
Hold to them, Father; don't let yourself be shaken.
Be careful lest your kind disposition
Induce you to abandon your position;
Cling to your resolutions, I entreat you,
And don't let Mother's stubbornness defeat you.

CHRYSALE

What! So you take me for a booby, eh?

HENRIETTE

Heavens, no!

CHRYSALE

Suis-je un fat, s'il vous plaît?

HENRIETTE

Je ne dis pas cela.

CHRYSALE

Me croit-on incapable
Des fermes sentiments d'un homme raisonnable?

HENRIETTE

Non, mon père.

CHRYSALE

Est-ce donc qu'à l'âge où je me vois
Je n'aurai pas l'esprit d'être maître chez moi?

HENRIETTE

Si fait[305].

CHRYSALE

Et que j'aurai cette faiblesse d'âme
De me laisser mener par le nez à ma femme?

HENRIETTE

Eh! non, mon père.

CHRYSALE

Am I a milksop, would you say?

HENRIETTE

I'd not say that.

CHRYSALE

Do you think I lack the sense
To stand up firmly for my sentiments?

HENRIETTE

No, Father.

CHRYSALE

Have I too little brain and spirit
To run my own house? If so, let me hear it.

HENRIETTE

No, no.

CHRYSALE

Am I the sort, do you suppose,
Who'd let a woman lead him by the nose?

HENRIETTE

Of course not.

CHRYSALE

Ouais! Qu'est-ce donc que ceci
Je vous trouve plaisante[306] à me parler ainsi.

HENRIETTE

Si je vous ai choqué, ce n'est pas mon envie.

CHRYSALE

Ma volonté céans doit être en tout suivie.

HENRIETTE

Fort bien, mon père.

CHRYSALE

Aucun, hors moi dans la maison
N'a droit de commander.

HENRIETTE

Oui, vous avez raison.

CHRYSALE

C'est moi qui tiens le rang de chef de la famille.

HENRIETTE

D'accord.

CHRYSALE

C'est moi qui dois disposer de ma fille.

CHRYSALE

Well then, what were you implying?
Your doubts of me were scarcely gratifying.

HENRIETTE

I didn't mean to offend you, Heaven knows.

CHRYSALE

Under this roof, my girl, what I say goes.

HENRIETTE

True, Father.

CHRYSALE

No one but me has any right
To govern in this house.

HENRIETTE

Yes, Father; quite.

CHRYSALE

This is my family, and I'm sole head.

HENRIETTE

That's so.

CHRYSALE

I'll name the man my child shall wed.

HENRIETTE

Eh! oui.

CHRYSALE

Le ciel me donne un plein pouvoir sur vous.

HENRIETTE

Qui vous dit le contraire?

CHRYSALE

Et, pour prendre un époux,
Je vous ferai bien voir que c'est à votre père
Qu'il vous faut obéir, non pas à votre mère.

HENRIETTE

Hélas! vous flattez là le plus doux de mes voeux;
Veuillez être obéi, c'est tout ce que je veux.

CHRYSALE

Nous verrons si ma femme, à mes désirs rebelle...

CLITANDRE

La voici qui conduit le notaire avec elle.

CHRYSALE

Secondez-moi bien tous.

HENRIETTE

Agreed!

CHRYSALE

By Heaven's laws, I rule your fate.

HENRIETTE

Who questions that?

CHRYSALE

And I'll soon demonstrate
That, in your marriage, your mother has no voice,
And that you must accept your father's choice.

HENRIETTE

Ah, Father, that's my dearest wish, I pray you,
Crown my desire by making me obey you.

CHRYSALE

If my contentious wife should dare to take—

CLITANDRE

She's coming, with the notary in her wake.

CHRYSALE

Stand by me, all of you.

LES FEMMES SAVANTES

MARTINE

Laissez-moi, j'aurai soin
De vous encourager, s'il en est besoin.

Act V   Scene Two

MARTINE

Trust me, Sir. I'm here
To back you up, if need be. Never fear.

Scène III

PHILAMINTE, BÉLISE, ARMANDE, TRISSOTIN, LE NOTAIRE, CHRYSALE,
CLITANDRE, HENRIETTE, MARTINE

PHILAMINTE (*au notaire*)

Vous ne sauriez changer votre style sauvage[307]
Et nous faire un contrat qui soit beau en langage?

LE NOTAIRE

Notre style est très bon, et je serais un sot,
Madame, de vouloir y changer un seul mot.

PHILAMINTE

Ah! quelle barbarie au milieu de la France!
Mais au moins, en faveur, monsieur, de la science,
Veuillez, au lieu d'écus, de livres et de francs,
Nous exprimer la dot en mines et talents[308]
Et dater par les mots d'ides et de calendes[309].

LE NOTAIRE

Moi? Si j'allais, madame, accorder vos demandes,
Je me ferais siffler de tous mes compagnons.

PHILAMINTE

De cette barbarie en vain nous nous plaignons.
Allons, monsieur; prenez la table pour écrire.
   (*Apercevant Martine*)
Ah! ah! cette imprudente[310] ose encor se produire?
Pourquoi donc, s'il vous plaît, la ramener chez moi?

Scene Three

PHILAMINTE, BÉLISE, ARMANDE, TRISSOTIN, THE NOTARY, CHRYSALE,
CLITANDRE, HENRIETTE, MARTINE

PHILAMINTE (*to the Notary*)

Can't you dispense with jargon, Sir, and write
Our contract in a style that's more polite?

THE NOTARY

Our style is excellent, Madam; I'd be absurd
Were I to modify a single word.

PHILAMINTE

Such barbarism, in the heart of France!
Can't you at least, for learning's sake, enhance
The document by putting the dowry down
In talent and drachma, rather than franc and crown?
And do use ides and calends for the date.

THE NOTARY

If I did, Madam, what you advocate,
I should invite professional ostracism.

PHILAMINTE

It's useless to contend with barbarism.
Come on, Sir; there's a writing table here.
          (*Noticing Martine*)
Ah! Impudent girl, how dare you reappear?
Why have you brought her back, Sir? Tell me why.

273

CHRYSALE

Tantôt avec loisir on vous dira pourquoi.
Nous avons maintenant autre chose à conclure.

LE NOTAIRE

Procédons au contrat. Où donc est la future?

PHILAMINTE

Celle que je marie est la cadette.

LE NOTAIRE

Bon.

CHRYSALE

Oui. La voilà, monsieur; Henriette est son nom.

LE NOTAIRE

Fort bien. Et le futur?

PHILAMINTE (*montrant Trissotin*)

L'époux que je lui donne
Est monsieur.

CHRYSALE (*montrant Clitandre*)

Et celui, moi, qu'en propre personne
Je prétends qu'elle épouse est monsieur.

CHRYSALE

I'll tell you that at leisure, by and by.
First, there's another matter to decide.

THE NOTARY

Let us proceed with the contract. Where's the bride?

PHILAMINTE

I'm giving away my younger daughter.

THE NOTARY

I see.

CHRYSALE

Yes. Henriette's her name, Sir. This is she.

THE NOTARY

Good. And the bridegroom?

PHILAMINTE (*indicating Trissotin*)

This is the man I choose.

CHRYSALE (*indicating Clitandre*)

And I, for my part, have a bit of news:
This is the man she'll marry.

LE NOTAIRE

Deux époux?
C'est trop pour la coutume[311].

PHILAMINTE

Où vous arrêtez-vous?
Mettez, mettez, monsieur, Trissotin pour mon gendre.

CHRYSALE

Pour mon gendre mettez, mettez, monsieur, Clitandre.

LE NOTAIRE

Mettez-vous donc d'accord, et, d'un jugement mûr,
Voyer à convenir entre vous du futur.

PHILAMINTE

Suivez, suivez, monsieur, le choix où je m'arrête.

CHRYSALE

Faites, faites, monsieur, les choses à ma tête.

LE NOTAIRE

Dites-moi donc à qui j'obéirai des deux.

PHILAMINTE (*à Chrysale*)

Quoi donc! vous combattez les choses que je veux?

Act V Scene Three

THE NOTARY

Two grooms? The law
Regards that as excessive.

PHILAMINTE

Don't hem and haw;
Just write down Trissotin, and your task is done.

CHRYSALE

Write down Clitandre; he's to be my son.

THE NOTARY

Kindly consult together, and agree
On a single person as the groom-to-be.

PHILAMINTE

No, no, Sir, do as I have indicated.

CHRYSALE

Come, come, put down the name that I have stated.

THE NOTARY

First tell me by whose orders I should abide.

PHILAMINTE (*to Chrysale*)

What's this, Sir? Shall my wishes be defied?

CHRYSALE

Je ne saurais souffrir qu'on ne cherche[312] ma fille
Que pour l'amour du bien qu'on voit dans ma famille.

PHILAMINTE

Vraiment, à votre bien on songe bien ici,
Et c'est là, pour un sage, un fort digne souci!

CHRYSALE

Enfin pour son époux j'ai fait choix de Clitandre.

PHILAMINTE (*montrant Trissotin*)

Et moi, pour son époux voici qui je veux prendre:
Mon choix sera suivi, c'est un point résolu.

CHRYSALE

Ouais! Vous le prenez là d'un ton bien absolu!

MARTINE

Ce n'est point à la femme à prescrire, et je sommes[313]
Pour céder le dessus en toute chose aux hommes.

CHRYSALE

C'est bien dit.

CHRYSALE

I won't stand by and let this fellow take
My daughter's hand just for my money's sake.

PHILAMINTE

A lot your money matters to him! Indeed!
How dare you charge a learnèd man with greed?

CHRYSALE

Clitandre shall marry her, as I said before.

PHILAMINTE (*pointing to Trissotin*)

This is the man I've chosen. I'll hear no more.
The matter's settled, do you understand?

CHRYSALE

My! For a woman, you have a heavy hand.

MARTINE

It just ain't right for the wife to run the shop.
The man, I say, should always be on top.

CHRYSALE

Well said.

MARTINE

Mon congé cent fois me fût-il hoc[314],
La poule ne doit point chanter devant le coq.

CHRYSALE

Sans doute.

MARTINE

Et nous voyons que d'un homme on se gausse
Quand sa femme chez lui porte le haut-de-chausse.

CHRYSALE

Il est vrai.

MARTINE

Si j'avais un mari, je le dis,
Je voudrais qu'il se fît le maître du logis.
Je ne l'aimerais point s'il faisait le Jocrisse[315];
Et, si je contestais contre lui par caprice,
Si je parlais trop haut, je trouverais fort bon
Qu'avec quelques soufflets il rabaissât mon ton.

CHRYSALE

C'est parler comme il faut.

MARTINE

Monsieur est raisonnable
De vouloir pour sa fille un mari convenable.

MARTINE

Though I'm sacked ten times for saying so,
It's cocks, not hens, should be the ones to crow.

CHRYSALE

Correct.

MARTINE

When a man's wife wears the breeches, folks
Snicker about him, and make nasty jokes.

CHRYSALE

That's true.

MARTINE

If I had a husband, I wouldn't wish
For him to be all meek and womanish;
No, no, he'd be the captain of the ship,
And if I happened to give him any lip,
Or crossed him, he'd be right to slap my face
A time or two, to put me in my place.

CHRYSALE

Sound thinking.

MARTINE

The master's heart is rightly set
On finding a proper man for Henriette.

CHRYSALE

Oui.

MARTINE

Par quelle raison, jeune et bien fait qu'il est,
Lui refuser Clitandre? Et pourquoi s'il vous plaît,
Lui bailler[316] un savant qui sans cesse épilogue?
Il lui faut un mari, non pas un pédagogue;
Et, ne voulant savoir le grais[317] ni le latin,
Elle n'a pas besoin de monsieur Trissotin.

CHRYSALE

Fort bien.

PHILAMINTE

Il faut souffrir qu'elle jase à son aise.

MARTINE

Les savants ne sont bons que pour prêcher en chaise;
Et pour mon mari, moi mille fois je l'ai dit,
Je ne voudrais jamais prendre un homme d'esprit.
L'esprit n'est point du tout ce qu'il faut en ménage;
Les livres cadrent mal avec le mariage;
Et je veux, si jamais on engage ma foi,
Un mari qui n'ait point d'autres livres que moi,
Qui ne sache A ne[317] B, n'en déplaise à madame,
Et ne soit, en un mot, docteur que pour sa femme.

CHRYSALE

Yes.

MARTINE

Well then, here's Clitandre. Why deny
The girl a fine young chap like him? And why
Give her a learnèd fool who prates and drones?
She needs a husband, not some bag of bones
Who'll teach her Greek, and be her Latin tutor.
This Trissotin, I tell you, just don't suit her.

CHRYSALE

Right.

PHILAMINTE

We must let her chatter until she's through.

MARTINE

Talk, talk, is all these pedants know how to do.
If I ever took a husband, I've always said,
It wouldn't be no learnèd man I'd wed.
Wit's not the thing you need around the house,
And it's no joy to have a bookish spouse.
When I get married, you can bet your life
My man will study nothing but his wife;
Hell have no other book to read but me,
And won't—so please you, Ma'am—know A from B.

PHILAMINTE (*à Chrysale*)

Est-ce fait? et sans trouble ai-je assez écouté
Votre indigne interprète?

CHRYSALE

Elle a dit vérité.

PHILAMINTE

Et moi pour trancher court toute cette dispute,
Il faut qu'absolument mon désir s'exécute.
Henriette et monsieur seront joints de ce pas[319];
Je l'ai dit, je le veux: ne me répliquez pas;
Et si votre parole à Clitandre est donnée,
Offrez-lui le parti d'épouser son aînée.

CHRYSALE

Voilà dans cette affaire un accommodement.
Voyez: y donnez-vous votre consentement?

HENRIETTE

Eh! mon père!

CLITANDRE

Eh! monsieur!

PHILAMINTE *(to Chrysale)*

Has your spokesman finished? And have I not politely
Listened to all her speeches?

CHRYSALE

The girl spoke rightly.

PHILAMINTE

Well then, to end all squabbling and delay,
things now shall go exactly as I say.
(*indicating Trissotin*)
Henriette shall wed this man at once, d'you hear?
Don't answer back; don't dare to interfere;
And if you've told Clitandre that he may wed
One of your daughters, give him Armande instead.

CHRYSALE

Well!... There's one way to settle this argument.
(*To Henriette and Clitandre*)
What do you think of that? Will you consent?

HENRIETTE

Oh, Father!

CLITANDRE

Oh, Sir!

BÉLISE

On pourrait bien lui faire
Des propositions qui pourraient mieux lui plaire;
Mais nous établissons une espèce d'amour
Qui doit être épuré comme l'astre du jour;
La substance qui pense y peut être reçue,
Mais nous en bannissons la substance étendue.

BÉLISE

There's yet another bride
By whom he might be yet more satisfied;
But that can't be; the love we share is far
Higher and purer than the morning star;
Our bonds are solely of the intellect,
And all extended substance we reject.

Scène IV

ARISTE, CHRYSALE, PHILAMINTE, BÉLISE, HENRIETTE, ARMANDE,
TRISSOTIN, LE NOTAIRE, CLITANDRE, MARTINE

ARISTE

J'ai regret de troubler un mystère[320] joyeux
Par le chagrin qu'il faut que j'apporte en ces lieux.
Ces deux lettres me font porteur de deux nouvelles
Dont j'ai senti pour vous les atteintes cruelles:
    (A Philaminte)
L'une pour vous me vient de votre procureur[321];
    (A Chrysale)
L'autre pour vous me vient de Lyon.

PHILAMINTE

           Quel malheur
Digne de nous troubler pourrait-on nous écrire?

ARISTE

Cette lettre en contient un que vous pouvez lire.

PHILAMINTE *(lit)*

"Madame, j'ai prié monsieur votre frère de vous rendre
cette lettre, qui vous dira ce que je n'ai osé vous aller dire.
La grande négligence que vous avez pour vos affaires a été
cause que le clerc de votre rapporteur ne m'a point averti,
et vous avez perdu absolument votre procès, que vous
deviez gagner."

SCENE FOUR

ARISTE, CHRYSALE, PHILAMINTE, BÉLISE, HENRIETTE, ARMANDE,
TRISSOTIN, THE NOTARY, CLITANDRE, MARTINE

ARISTE

I hate to interrupt this happy affair
By bringing you the tidings which I bear.
You can't imagine what distress I feel
At the shocking news these letters will reveal.
(*To Philaminte*)
This one's from your attorney.
(*To Chrysale*)
And the other is yours; it's from Lyons.

PHILAMINTE

What news, dear Brother,
Could be so pressing, and distress you so?

ARISTE

There is your letter; read it, and you'll know.

PHILAMINTE (*reading*)

"Madam, I have asked your brother to convey to you this
message advising you of something which I dared not come
and tell you in person. Owing to your great neglect of your
affairs, the magistrate's clerk did not notify me of the
preliminary hearing, and you have irrevocably lost your
lawsuit, which you should in fact have won."

CHRYSALE (*à Philaminte*)

Votre procès perdu!

PHILAMINTE

Vous vous troublez beaucoup!
Mon coeur n'est point du tout ébranlé de ce coup.
Faites, faites paraître une âme moins commune
A braver comme moi les traits de la fortune.
"Le peu de soin que vous avez vous coûte quarante mille
écus, et c'est à payer cette somme, avec les dépens, que vous
êtes condamnée par arrêt de la cour."
Condamnée! Ah! ce mot est choquant et n'est fait
Que pour les criminels.

ARISTE

Il a tort, en effet,
Et vous vous êtes là justement récriée.
Il devrait avoir mis que vous êtes priée
Par arrêt de la cour de payer au plus tôt
Quarante mille écus et les dépens qu'il faut.

PHILAMINTE

Voyons l'autre.

CHRYSALE *(lit)*

"Monsieur, l'amitié qui me lie à monsieur votre frère
me fait prendre intérêt à tout ce qui vous touche. Je sais
que vous avez mis votre bien entre les mains d'Argante
et de Damon, et je vous donne avis qu'en même jour ils
ont fait tous deux banqueroute[322]."
O ciel! tout à la fois perdre ainsi tout mon bien!

CHRYSALE (*to Philaminte*)

You've lost your case!

PHILAMINTE

My! Don't be shaken so!
I'm not disheartened by this trivial blow.
Do teach your heart to take a nobler stance
And brave, like me, the buffetings of chance.
"This negligence of yours has cost you forty thousand
crowns, for it is that amount, together with the legal
expenses, which the court has condemned you to pay."
Condemned! What shocking language! That's a word
Reserved for criminals.

ARISTE

True; your lawyer erred,
And you're entirely right to be offended.
He should say that the court has *recommended*
That you comply with its decree, and pay
Forty thousand and costs without delay.

PHILAMINTE

What's in this other letter?

CHRYSALE (*reading*)

"Sir, my friendship with your brother leads me to take
an interest in all that concerns you. I know that you have
put your money in the hands of Argante and Damon, and
I regret to inform you that they have both, on the same day,
gone into bankruptcy."
Lost! All my money! Every penny of it!

PHILAMINTE

Ah! quel honteux transport! Fi! tout cela n'est rien.
Il n'est pour le vrai sage aucun revers funeste,
Et, perdant toute chose, à soi-même il se reste.
Achevons notre affaire, et quittez votre ennui[323]:
   (Montrant Trissotin)
Son bien peut nous suffire et pour nous et pour lui.

TRISSOTIN

Non, madame cessez de presser cette affaire.
Je vois qu'à cet hymen tout le monde est contraire,
Et mon dessein n'est point de contraindre les gens.

PHILAMINTE

Cette réflexion vous vient en peu de temps!
Elle suit de bien près, monsieur, notre disgrâce[324].

TRISSOTIN

De tant de résistance à la fin je me lasse,
J'aime mieux renoncer à tout cet embarras
Et ne veux point d'un coeur qui ne se donne pas.

PHILAMINTE

Je vois, je vois de vous, non pas pour votre gloire,
Ce que jusques ici j'ai refusé de croire.

PHILAMINTE

What a shameful outburst, Sir. Come, rise above it!
The wise man doesn't mourn the loss of pelf;
His wealth lies not in things, but in himself.
Let's finish this affair, with no more fuss:
   (*Pointing to Trissotin*)
His fortune will suffice for all of us.

TRISSOTIN

No, Madam, urge my case no further. I see
That everyone's against this match and me,
And where I am not wanted, I shan't intrude.

PHILAMINTE

Well! That's a sudden change of attitude.
It follows close on our misfortunes, Sir.

TRISSOTIN

Weary of opposition, I prefer
To bow out gracefully, and to decline
A heart which will not freely yield to mine.

PHILAMINTE

I see now what you are, Sir. I perceive
What, till this moment, I would not believe.

TRISSOTIN

Vous pouvez voir de moi tout ce que vous voudrez
Et je regarde peu comment vous le prendrez;
Mais je ne suis point homme à souffrir l'infamie
Des refus offensants qu'il faut qu'ici j'essuie:
Je vaux bien que de moi l'on fasse plus de cas,
Et je baise les mains[325] à qui ne me veut pas.
   (Il sort)

PHILAMINTE

Qu'il a bien découvert son âme mercenaire!
Et que peu philosophe est ce qu'il vient de faire!

CLITANDRE

Je ne me vante point de l'être; mais enfin
Je m'attache, madame, à tout votre destin;
Et j'ose vous offrir, avecque[326] ma personne,
Ce qu'on sait que de bien la fortune me donne.

PHILAMINTE

Vous me charmez, monsieur, par ce trait généreux,
Et je veux couronner vos désirs amoureux.
Oui, j'accorde Henriette à l'ardeur empressée...

HENRIETTE

Non, ma mère, je change à présent de pensée.
Souffrez que je résiste à votre volonté.

CLITANDRE

Quoi! vous vous opposez à ma félicité?
Et, lorsqu'à mon amour je vois chacun se rendre...

TRISSOTIN

See what you like; I do not care one whit
What you perceive, or what you think of it.
I've too much self-respect to tolerate
The rude rebuffs I've suffered here of late:
Men of my worth should not be treated so:
Thus slighted, I shall make my bow, and go.
     (*He leaves*)

PHILAMINTE

What a low-natured, mercenary beast!
He isn't a philosophic in the least!

CLITANDRE

Madam, I'm no philosopher; but still
I beg to share your fortunes, good or ill,
And dare to offer, together with my hand,
The little wealth I happen to command.

PHILAMINTE

This generous gesture, Sir, I much admire,
And you deserve to have your heart's desire.
I grant you suit, Sir. Henriette and you—

HENRIETTE

No, Mother, I've changed my mind. Forgive me, do,
If once more I oppose your plans for me.

CLITANDRE

What! Will you cheat me of felicity,
Now that the rest have yielded, one and all?

HENRIETTE

Je sais le peu de bien que vous avez, Clitandre,
Et je vous ai toujours souhaité pour époux,
Lorsqu'en satisfaisant à mes voeux les plus doux
J'ai vu que mon hymen ajustait[327] vos affaires;
Mais, lorsque nous avons les destins si contaires,
Je vous chéris assez, dans cette extrémité,
Pour ne vous charger point de notre adversité.

CLITANDRE

Tout destin avec vous me peut être agréable;
Tout destin me serait sans vous insupportable.

HENRIETTE

L'amour dans son transport parle toujours ainsi.
Des retours[328] importuns évitons le souci.
Rien n'use tant l'ardeur de ce noeud qui nous lie
Que les fâcheux besoins des choses de la vie,
Et l'on vient souvent à s'accuser tous deux
De tous les noirs chagrins qui suivent de tels feux.

ARISTE (à *Henriette*)

N'est-ce que le motif que nous venons d'entendre
Qui vous fait résister à l'hymen de Clitandre?

HENRIETTE

Sans cela, vous verriez tout mon coeur y courir;
Et je ne fuis sa main que pour le trop chérir[329].

HENRIETTE

I know, Clitandre, that your wealth is small.
I wished to marry you so long as I
Might realize my sweetest hopes thereby,
And at the same time mend your circumstances.
But after this great blow to our finances,
I love you far too deeply to impose
On you the burden of our present woes.

CLITANDRE

I welcome any fate which you will share,
And any fate, without you, I couldn't bear.

HENRIETTE

So speaks the reckless heart of love; but let's
Be prudent, Sir, and thus avoid regrets.
Nothing so strains the bond of man and wife
As lacking the necessities of life,
And in the end, such dull and mean vexations
Can lead to quarrels and recriminations.

ARISTE (*to Henriette*)

Is there any reason, save the one you've cited,
Why you and Clitandre shouldn't be united?

HENRIETTE

But for that cause, I never would say no;
I must refuse because I love him so.

ARISTE

Laissez-vous donc lier par des chaînes si belles.
Je ne vous ai porté que de fausses nouvelles,
Et c'est un stratagème, un surprenant secours,
Que j'ai voulu tenter pour servir vos amours,
Pour détromper ma soeur et lui faire connaître
Ce que son philosophe à l'essai[330] pouvait être.

CHRYSALE

Le ciel en soit loué!

PHILAMINTE

        J'en ai la joie au coeur
Par le chagrin qu'aura ce lâche déserteur.
Voilà le châtiment de sa basse avarice,
De voir qu'avec éclat cet hymen s'accomplisse.

CHRYSALE (à *Clitandre*)

Je le savais bien, moi, que vous l'épouseriez.

ARMANDE (à *Philaminte*)

Ainsi donc à leurs voeux vous me sacrifiez!

PHILAMINTE

Ce ne sera point vous que je leur sacrifie,
Et vous avez l'appui de la philosophie
Pour voir d'un oeil content couronner leur ardeur.

Act V SCENE FOUR

ARISTE

Then let the bells ring out for him and you.
The bad news which I brought was all untrue.
'Twas but a strategem which I devised
In hopes to see your wishes realized
And undeceive my sister, showing her
The baseness of her pet philosopher.

CHRYSALE

Now, Heaven be praised for that!

PHILAMINTE

I'm overjoyed
To think how that false wretch will be annoyed,
And how the rich festivites of this
Glad marriage will torment his avarice.

CHRYSALE (*to Clitandre*)

Well, Son, our firmness has achieved success.

ARMANDE (*to Philaminte*)

Shall you sacrifice me to their happiness?

PHILAMINTE

Daughter, your sacrifice will not be hard.
Philosophy will help you to regard
Their wedded joys with equanamity.

BÉLISE

Qu'il prenne garde au moins que je suis dans son coeur.
Par un prompt désespoir souvent on se marie,
Qu'on s'en repent après tout le temps de sa vie.

CHRYSALE (*au notaire*)

Allons, monsieur, suivez l'ordre que j'ai prescrit,
Et faites le contrat ainsi que je l'ai dit.

Act V SCENE FOUR

BÉLISE

Let him be careful lest his love for me
Drive him, in desperation, to consent
To a rash marriage of which he will repent.

CHRYSALE (*to the Notary*)

Come, come, Sir, it is time your task was through;
Draw up the contract just as I told you to.

Annotations

NB   con.fr = contemporary French definition

Personnages
bon bourgeois - of the well-to-do middle class

Scène I

1.   **fille** - normally seen as *jeune fille* or an unmarried young woman
2.   **faire fête** - to look forward with pleasure (con.fr = celebrate)
3.   **vulgaire** - banal or common
4.   **sans un mal de coeur** - without becoming sick
5.   **dégoûtant** - without taste (con.fr = disgusting)
6.   **résoudre** - to make (your heart) accept
7.   **attachements** - bonds or ties
8.   **bien assorti** - if well matched
9.   **appas** - charms
10. **étage** - level
11. **vous claquemurer** - to shut you up in
12. **un idole** - now feminine, *une idole.* The gender of some nouns was not fixed in the 17th century.
13. **des marmots** - monkey-like, rather grotesque
14. **amusements** - In the 17th century, *amusement* suggested an activity that was a waste of time, or at least an unnecessary diversion.
15. **prendre un goût** - In modern French: *prendre goût à*
16. **de mépris** - *avec mépris*
17. **clartés** - knowledge, or intellectual pursuits
18. **vous rendez** - In the 17th century, an object pronoun often preceded a verb in the imperative form.
19. **l'empire** - power (con.fr = sway)
20. **ravale** - lowers
21. **beaux feux** - strong fervor
22. **Me paraissent aux yeux** - *paraissent à mes yeux*, seems to me
23. **aux élévations** - noble ideas
24. **génie** - talent, or disposition (con.fr = genius)
25. **l'hymen** - marriage

26. **aux productions** - *dans les productions*
27. **bien vous prend** - it is lucky for you
28. **N'ait pas vaqué** - was not devoted
29. **souffrez-moi** - allow me
30. **la clarté** - literally translated the light of day, i.e. your birth
31. **faire** - to find
32. **malhonnête** - lacking in courtesy (con.fr = dishonest or rude)
33. **hautement** - clearly, publically (con.fr = loudly)
34. **un mérite** - a meritorious person
35. **croi** - *crois:* The elimination of the "s" results from the poetic license to rhyme visually with *foi.*
36. **si bonne foi** - naive belief

Scène II

37. **nous daignez** - Another example of the 17th century usage of an object pronoun placed before a verb in the imperative.
38. **comme** - *combien* or how much
39. **madame** - In the 17th century, this form of address could be used for unmarried women of high social standing.
40. **pas** - situation
41. **joug** - domination
42. **traits** - glances or looks. In the love poetry of the 16th century, it was said that a woman's eyes can shoot arrows directly into the heart of her lover.
43. **pitoyable** - full of pity
44. **le rebut de vos charmes** - what your charms have rejected
45. **essayer à** - *essayer de*
46. **l'on** - *je*, Armande's use of the impersonal pronoun is ironic.
47. **plaisant** - comical, or even ridiculous
48. **Sans le congé** - Without the permission
49. **l'agrément** - approval
50. **me donnez** - Another example of an object pronoun preceding an imperative: *donnez-moi.*
51. **hautement** - openly
52. **chagrin** - irritation (con.fr = sorrow or trouble)

Scène III

53. **hauteurs** - snobby manifestations (con.fr = arrogance)
54. **humeur** - temperament
55. **d'abord** - immediately (con.fr = first and foremost)

56. **visions** - crazy ideas (con.fr = fantasies)
57. **les femmes docteurs** - Women who have completed the highest level of university study, i.e. those with the equivalent of a Ph.D. degree.
58. **je veux qu'elle se cache** - Literally, I want her to hide herself. Figuratively in this context it means I want her to keep her knowledge in the background.
59. **Aux encens** - To the compliments
60. **on siffle** - one mocks (con.fr = hiss or boo; whistling was a sign of disapproval)
61. **la plume libérale** - copious pen, i.e. he writes too much
62. **D'officieux papiers fournir la halle** - Trissotin's papers are useful to wrap up food at the city market.
63. **et vos yeux** - i.e. I have the same perspective on things.
64. **à sa flamme contraire** - against his love
65. **avant que** - *avant de*
66. **soi-même** - *lui-même*
67. **Qu'il se sait si bon gré de** - he congratulates himself
68. **encor** - Elimination of final "e" for the prosody, a poetic license.
69. **le Palais** - The entryway to the Palais de Justice, or Court House, was lined with different kinds of shops, including bookstalls, where writers and fashionable people often met.
70. **mystère** - secret (con.fr = mystery)

Scène IV

71. **se découvre à vous de** - reveals to you
72. **tout beau!** - gently
73. **chez moi** - *selon moi*, or in my opinion
74. **flammes** - desires (con.fr = flames or passion)
75. **aux muets interprêtes** - i.e. the eyes, amorous looks
76. **d'esprit** - ingenious, (con. fr. = the spirit of, i.e. *l'esprit de corps*)
77. **faux-fuyant** - subterfuge
78. **son aimable empire** - in her power to inspire love
79. **l'hymen d'Henriette** - marriage with Henriette
80. **j'entende** - *je comprenne*, I understand
81. **la figure** - the image
82. **sans rien prétendre** - with no hope (con.fr = claiming nothing)
83. **embarras** - complication
84. **point de façons** - no need for such complications
85. **l'on est** - *je sois*, The Précieuses often used the impersonal form, *on*, to suggest a sense of modesty.

86. **la figure** - figure of speech
87. **transports** - expressions (con.fr = emotional outburst)
88. **autels** - i.e. to me as a shrine of a love cult
89. **Diantre** - A deformation of *diable*, which people avoided saying for fear of sacrilege.
90. **préventions** - preconceived ideas (con.fr = bias)
91. **commetre un autre au soin** - to put someone else in charge of the help

ACTE II

Scène II

92. **Dieu vous gard'** - A common greeting. The apostrophe indicates that the "e" has been elided, even though the old form of the subjunctive of this verb had no "e" in this form.
93. **estime** - opinion, either good or bad
94. **de conduite** - of forethought
95. **verts galants** - wild young men
96. **Nous donnions chez** - We were passionate for

Scène III

97. **en est charmé** - in love with her, i.e. under her charm
98. **abuse vos esprits** - is deceiving you
99. **Hai** - An exclamation expressing amusement
100. **d'un air** - appearance
101. **Qu'on n'a pas pour un coeur** - That I dont have merely one lover
102. **licence** - liberty
103. **céans** - into this house, here
104. **piquants** - hurtful (con.fr = stinging) In modern usage it usually refers to a painful, sensation, stinging.
105. **vision toute claire** - purely and simply an illusion

Scène IV

106. **oui** - Has the meaning of "indeed" in this phrase
107. **le discours** - the subject of the conversation
108. **un intérêt** - a problem, or a matter
109. **aux choses de ce pas** - what we've decided upon

Scène V

110. **chanceuse** - lucky
111. **Qui veut noyer son chien l'accuse de rage** - A French proverb with the literal meaning of "Whoever wants to drown his dog claims that he has rabies."
112. **bailler** - to give

Scène VI

113. **maraude** - riff-raff
114. **Tout doux!** - Gently! Easy does it!
115. **Suis-je pour** - Am I capable of?
116. **Aussi fais-je** - That's what I'm going to do
117. **Coquine** - rascal, dishonest person
118. **Me voit-on** - Am I considered?
119. **aiguière** - a large vase with a handle to pour water into a sink before washing one's hands
120. **fidèle** - honest (con.fr = loyal) In modern usage it means loyal.
121. **insulté** - scorched (con.fr = insulted)
122. **Vaugelas** - The predominant authority in the 17th century on correct grammar and good taste. His *Remarques sur la langue française* (1647) attempts to reform and codify the French language once and for all.
123. **lois** - rules of grammar
124. **Je n'ai garde** - I have no such intention
125. **le bel usage** - According to Vaugelas, proper usage was modeled upon the language spoken at the royal court: *"la façon de parler de la plus saine partie de la cour, conformément à la façon d'écrire de la plus saine partie des auteurs du temps."*
126. **biaux dictons** - fine sayings. *Biaux* is a peasant deformation of *beaux*.
127. **congrûment** - properly
128. **je n'avons pas étugué** - Use of a plural verb with a singular pronoun and a rustic pronunciation of *étudié*.
129. **cheux** - *chez:* Another example of Martine's rustic pronunciation.
130. **grandmère** - In the 17th century, one pronounced *grammaire* like *grandmère*, thus Martine's comic confusion.
131. **Chaillot, d'Auteuil ou de Pontoise** - Different areas of Paris.
132. **se gourment** - have a fistfight (con.fr = to strangle each other)

Scène VII

133. **sortie** - dismissal
134. **vices d'oraison** - mistakes in language
135. **les ruisseaux des halles** - i.e. the uncouth speech of market vendors
136. **ce grossier génie** - this base mind
137. **le pléonasme ou la cacaphonie** - Terms used to describe language that is redundant in meaning (pleonasm) or harsh sounding (cacaphony).
138. **méchant** - bad
139. **Malherbe et Balzac** - François de Malherbe (1566-1628), admired by such critics as Boileau for his reforms of French poetry at the beginning of the 17th century, is often considered the great leader of the French classical school. Jean-Louis Guez de Balzac (1597-1654) created a refined prose style that was received enthusiastically in the literary salons of the period.
140. **homme** - refers to/defines all humanity or human beings in general
141. **fait figure** - forms an ensemble
142. **instance** - endeavor
143. **viande bien creuse** - food with no substance in it
144. **collet monté** - out-of-fashion, outdated, or even stilted. A *collet monté* was a stiff collar, fashioned on a framework of wire and cardboard. It was no longer in use in 1672.
145. **décharge ma rate** - vent my anger. In the 17th century, the spleen supposedly contained a liquid that created anger or a bad mood.
146. **solécisme en parlant** - a grammatical mistake when someone speaks
147. **un gros Plutarque** - i.e. a heavy folio edition of Plutarch that Chrysale finds useful to press his collars (*rabats*)
148. **ce meuble inutile** - this useless stuff
149. **ses gens** - her servants, or household help
150. **un haut-de-chausse** - underwear that descended to the knees
151. **comme** - *comment*
152. **ne font rien moins que** - do anything but
153. **la raison** - here, good sense
154. **A cause qu'elle** - *Parce qu'elle*
155. **tympanisées** - has made you famous (like beating on a drum)
156. **bilevesées** - foolishness
157. **le timbre un peu fêlé** - a little cracked in the brain
158. **petits corps** - atoms, or molecules, in the philosophical jargon of the disciples of Lucretius

159. **bourgeois** - here, commonplace, unrefined
160. **veux mal de mort** - highly indignant. Belisle, prone to exaggeration, is "deadly" angry with herself.

Scène IX

161. **la femme** - a familiar way of saying "your wife"
162. **le succès** - outcome
163. **le bruit** - quarreling
164. **avecque** - an archaic form of *avec*
165. **grand mystère** - a real fuss
166. **le bien** - material wealth
167. **en bête** - like a fool
168. **comme on vous nomme** - how you are treated
169. **immoler** - sacrifice
170. **à tout coup** - all the time
171. **à la barbe des gens** - right in their face

ACTE III

Scène I

172. **brûlé** - burning with impatience
173. **Hélas** - An interjection of false modesty
174. **d'accoucher** - to write, or to create. Trissotin wants to extend his metaphor of a newborn (*un enfant tout nouveau-né*).

Scène II

175. **sciences** - knowledge in general
176. **l'impertinent** - clumsy fellow
177. **Bien lui prend** - It's lucky for him
178. **madrigal** - A short love poem
179. **le ragoût** - seasoning, or relish
180. **sel attique** - A reference to Athens, famous for its schools of rhetoric
181. **entêtement** - passion
182. **Uranie** - This sonnet was actually written by l'abbé Cotin and published in his *Oeuvres galantes*. It was addressed to Mlle de Longueville, the duchesse de Nemours.
183. **die** - an old form of the subjunctive *dise*
184. **De votre riche appartement** - i.e. in your fair body
185. **impayable** - priceless
186. **coquets** - malicious gossip

187. **tiercets** - *tercets*: A sonnet is composed of two quatrains of four lines each and two tercets of three lines each.
188. **se prend** - attacks
189. **marchander** - to humor someone (con.fr = to bargain with someone)
190. **Amies** - This is also a genuine poem of l'abbé Cotin, but its real title is "*Sur un carrosse de couleur amarante acheté par une dame, madrigal.*"
191. **Lais** - The name of a Greek courtesan, admired for her beauty.
192. **L'enveloppe** - allusion or symbol
193. **se décline** - is declined. A reference to Latin grammar, in which nouns are declined according to their function in a sentence.
194. **prévenu** - biased
195. **Platon** - Philaminte refers to Plato's *Republic*, in which the Greek philosopher describes an ideal society. She expects to realize such a place based on the emancipation of women.
196. **De borner** - to limit
197. **clartés** - knowledge in general. But Philaminte is criticizing also the refusal of the Académie française and the Académie des sciences to admit women as members.
198. **hors de page** - In the Middle Ages, when a page became old enough to be a squire, he was declared independent, thus emancipated.
199. **des ordres meilleurs** - better regulations
200. **qu'on sépare ailleurs** - Philaminte favors a single academy that would combine humanities and the sciences and would train women as well as men.
201. **péripatétisme** - The philosphy of Aristotle, based on logic and the scientific method
202. **le platonisme** - The idealism of Plato
203. **Epicure** - Epicurius, the Greek philosopher, created a system of atomic philosophy, thus Bélise's reference in the next verse to *petits corps*, or atoms.
204. **Descartes** - The French philosopher (1596-1650) believed that subtle matter (*la matière subtile*) filled the space between bodies and prevented a vacuum. Likewise, *tourbillons*, or vortices, is a term of Cartesian philosophy that indicates the whirling motion of planets around the sun. *Mondes tombants* are comets, or shooting stars.
205. **des hommes dans la lune** - That people inhabited the moon was a fairly common belief in the 17th century.

206. **sage** - The stoical "Wise Person" who loved virtue and scorned unhappiness.
207. **des remuements** - reforms
208. **juste ou naturelle** - rational or instinctive
209. **nous nous abandonnons** - we have agreed to discard
210. **et ne verrons que nous qui sache bien écrire** - *Et nous ne verrons personne d'autre que nous qui sache bien écrire* which helps to understand why *sache* is in the 3rd person singular: the *qui* refers to an understood *personne*.

Scène III

211. **produisant** - *présentant*, in the manner of presenting/producing a play
212. **tenir son coin** - hold his own, an expression from tennis, referring to an ability to return services
213. **fâcheux** - disagreeable
214. **j'aurai pu troubler** - I may be disturbing
215. **au palais, au cours, aux ruelles** - The Palais de Justice with its shops and bookstalls and the Cours-la-Reine, a fashionable promenade. *Ruelles* were small passageways between the bed and the walls. In the 17th century, ladies received their guests in their rooms and placed them on seats in these passageways, while they reclined comfortably on the bed.
216. **gueuser des encens** - to beg for compliments
217. **les Martyrs de ses veilles** - the martyrs of his vigils
218. **'lithos' et le 'pathos'** - manners and emotions, terms from classical rhetoric
219. **Theocrite et Virgile** - Theocritus, a Greek poet, and Virgil, a Latin poet, were both famous for their pastoral verse.
220. **Horace** - Latin poet who wrote many odes
221. **bouts-rimés**- *Rondeaux, madrigaux, ballades*, and *bout-rimés* are different verse forms popular in the 17th century.
222. **grimaud** - a scribbler
223. **rimeur de balle** - A writer of verses who carries them around in a pack (*balle*) and tries to peddle them off on people.
224. **fripier d'écrits** - A secondhand dealer in writings, i.e. a literary hack.
225. **Parnasse** - A mountain in Greece where, supposedly, lived Apollo, the god of poetry, and the Muses.
226. **Satires** - The work of Nicolas Boileau (1638-1711), a friend of Molière and a noteworthy critic.

227. **il ne te laisse pas en paix** -Boileau had indeed attacked l'abbé Cotin several times in his writings.

228. **Barbin** - A well-known bookstore among the shops in the Palais de Justice and the editor of Boileau and Moliére.

Scène IV

229. **que je vous détermine** - I oblige you

230. **Tout beau** - Easy does it

Scène V

231. **honnête** - suitable

Scène VI

232. **ce gant** - Women of high society wore gloves when they greeted people, even in their own home.

233. **le soûl** - till you're full

ACTE IV

Scène I

234. **fait vanité de son obéissance** - received great pride from obeying (her father)

235. **la forme ou la matière** - The soul (*forme*) organizes and animates the body (*matière*), according to Aristotle.

236. **un compliment** - A compliment, in this case, refers to courteous treatment.

237. **prié** - In contemporary French, the past participle agrees in gender and number with a preceding direct object. We would expect *priée*.

Scène II

238. **si j'étais que de vous** - *si j'étais vous*

239. **d'avoir quelque pensée** - if one would dare think

240. **discourant** - when we used to talk (con.fr = airing one's opinions)

241. **Le brutal** - the impolite man

242. **d'honnêteté** - consideration

243. **lautoriser** - to justify it

244. **ou si** - *ou est-ce que*

245. **d'une amour grossière** - a love without any elegance. In the 17th century, *amour* could be masculine or feminine in the singular.

246. **ardeurs** - desires

247. **dénié** - refused

248. **avec tout moi-même** - with body and soul (or "all of myself")
249. **je résous mon esprit** - I make my mind
250. **retour** - reversal, recantation
251. **fiertés** - cruelties
252. **Hors céans** - Outside of this place

Scène III
253. **échappé belle** - a narrow escape
254. **Un monde** - a comet. L'abbé Cotin had written a *Galanteries sur la comète apparue en décembre 1664 et janvier 1665*
255. **soit pour** - is able to
256. **maximes** - principles
257. **Le savoir dans un fat devient impertinent** - Knowledge in a fool becomes out of place.
258. **rude** - formidable (con.fr = severe)
259. **second** - a "second" in a duel
260. **Il entend raillerie** - he understands the joke
261. **sa gloire** - his reputation, or his self-esteem
262. **que j'essuie** - which I am facing
263. **c'est tout dit** - that's it in a nutshell
264. **Vous en voulez beaucoup** - You have a lot against
265. **vos méchants succès** - your bad results
266. **se connaître à tout** - to know something about everything
267. **Rasius et Baldus** - fictional scholars
268. **gredins** - miserable beggars
269. **pour être imprimés** - *parce qu'ils sont imprimés;* because they are printed
270. **impertinence** - foolishness

Scène IV
271. **gens** - servants, or domestic help
272. **Catulle** - Terence and Catullus were famous Latin poets
273. **l'effet** - realisation
274. **lui dites** - Another example of an object pronoun preceding a verb in the imperative
275. **assister** - to be present
276. **d'envoyer au notaire** - to send someone for the notary
277. **visées** - projects

Scène V
278. **de rimer à latin** - *rimer avec latin* i.e. to write Latin verse
279. **quand j'aurai son appui** - as long as I have his support
280. **une retraite** - a convent

ACTE V

Scène I
281. **ou** - *auquel*
282. **un bien** - wealth
283. **mais je n'y puis que faire** - I can't help it
284. **me vouloir mal** - to be angry at myself
285. **voeux** - feelings (con.fr = wishes)
286. **honnête homme** - honorable man
287. **cher** - dear in the sense of valuable
288. **aimable** - lovable
289. **galimatias** - incomprehensible language, gibberish
290. **d'Amarantes** - These three are conventional names used by poets to designate the women they love
291. **charmant** - captivating
292. **à vous le trancher net** - to tell you plainly
293. **en dépit qu'elle en ait** - in spite of herself
294. **altéré** - worried about
295. **n'ait pas pour** - i.e. is not likely
296. **constamment** - with constancy
297. **à vous si singulière** - particular to you alone
298. **qui prenne** - *quelqu'un qui prenne*
299. **sa gloire** - his reputation
300. **bien** - good fortune

Scène II
301. **à vivre** - how to behave
302. **malgré ses dents** - against her wishes
303. **à vos bontés** - by your kindliness
304. **l'emporte** - wins out
305. **Si fait** - On the contrary
306. **plaisante** - ridiculous

Scène III
307. **sauvage** - uncouth
308. **en mines et talents** - Greek coins
309. **d'ides et de calendes** - dates of the Roman calendar (ides: 13th or 15th of the month; calendes: 1st day of the month)
310. **impudente**- insolent person
311. **la coutume** - the law
312. **cherche** - seeks to marry
313. **je sommes** - *je suis*: Martine again uses a plural form of this with a singular subject
314. **hoc** - certain; The word derives from a card game in which the winning card was greeted with a *hoc*.
315. **la Jocrisse** - a stock figure in comedy, often ridiculed and always beat upon
316. **bailler** - *donner*
317. **le grais** - an old pronunciaton of *le grec*
318. **ne** - *ni*
319. **de ce pas** - right now

Scène IV
320. **mystère** - ceremony
321. **procureur** - another word for *avocat* (lawyer)
322. **banqueroute** - bankruptcy
323. **ennui** - dismay
324. **disgrâce** - misfortune (con.fr = disgrace)
325. **je baise les mains** - A common way of saying goodbye, used sarcastically here by Trissotin.
326. **avecque** - an archaic spelling, permissible in verse
327. **ajustant** - arranged
328. **retours** - regrets
329. **pour le trop chérir** - because I cherish him too much
330. **à l'essai** - when put to the test

For Further Reading

Adam, Antoine. *Histoire de la littérature française au XVIIe siècle.* Tome III. Paris: Domat, 1952.

Bénichou, Paul. *Morales du grand siècle.* Paris: Gallimard, 1948.

Bermel, Albert. *Molière's Theatrical Bounty: A New View of the Plays.* Carbondale: Southern Illinois University Press, 1990.

Bray, René. *Molière, homme de théâtre.* Paris: Mercure de France, 1954.

Cairncross, John, ed. *L'Humanité de Molière.* Paris: Librairie Nizet, 1988.

Carmody, James P. *Re-reading Molière: mise en scène from Antoine to Vitez.* Ann Arbor: University of Michigan Press, 1993.

Dandrey, Patrick. *Molière ou l'esthétique du ridicule.* Paris: Klincksieck, 1992.

Defaux, Gérard. *Molière ou les métamorphoses du comique: de la comédie morale au triomphe de la folie.* 2nd edition. Paris: Klincksieck, 1992.

Garapon, Robert. *Le dernier Molière: des "Fourberies de Scapin" au "Malade imaginaire."* Paris: Société d'édition d'enseignement supérieur, 1977.

Gossman, Lionel. *Men and Masks: A Study of Molière.* Baltimore: John Hopkins University Press, 1963.

Gross, Nathan. *From Gesture to Idea—Esthetics and Ethics in Molière's Comedy.* New York: Columbia University Press, 1982.

Guicharnaud, Jacques, ed. *Molière. A Collection of Critical Essays.* Englewood Cliffs, NJ: Prentice-Hall, 1964.

Hall, H. Gaston. *Comedy in Context: Essays on Molière.* Jackson: University of Mississippi Press, 1984.

Howarth, W.D. *Molière: A Playwrite and His Audience.* Cambridge: Cambridge University Press, 1982.

Jurgens, Madeleine, and Elizabeth Maxfield-Miller. *Cent ans de recherche sur Molière.* Paris: Imprimerie nationale, 1963.

Lawrence, Francis L. *Molière: The Comedy of Unreason.* New Orleans: Tulane University Press, 1968.

Lough, John. *An Introduction to Seventeenth-Century France.* New York: McKay, 1969.

Moore, Will. *Molière: A New Criticism.* Oxford: Clarendon Press, 1949.

Mornet, Daniel. *Molière.* 4th edition. Paris: Hatier-Boivin, 1943.

Reynier, Gustave. *"Les Femmes savantes" de Molière: étude et analyse.*
Paris: Melottee, 1936.
Simon, Alfred. *Molière, une vie.* Lyon: La Manufacture, 1987.
Walker, Hallam. *Molière.* New York: Twayne, 1971.

French Language Titles
from Hippocrene . . .

MASTERING FRENCH
by E.J. Neather
A useful tool for language learning, this method combines a full-size text with two audio cassettes allowing learners to hear proper pronunciation by native speakers as they study the book.
Book: 288 pages, 5 ½ x 8 ½, 0-87052-055-5
$11.95pb (511)
2 Cassettes: 0-87052-060-1
$12.95 (512)

MASTERING ADVANCED FRENCH
by E.J. Neather
An advanced course of French utilizing the method of *Mastering French..*
Book: 278 pages, 5 ½ x 8 ½, 0-7818-0312-8
$14.95 pb (41)
2 Cassettes; 0-7818-0313-6
$12.95 (54)

FRENCH HANDY DICTIONARY
For the traveler of independent spirit and curious mind, this practical dictionary will help you to communicate, not just get by. Common phrases are conveniently listed through key words. Pronunciation follows each entry and a reference section reviews all major grammar points.
120 pages, 5 x 8 , 0-7818-0010-2
$8.95 pb (155)

FRENCH-ENGLISH/ENGLISH-FRENCH
PRACTICAL DICTIONARY With Larger Print
by Rosalind Williams
35,000 entries, 386 pages, 5 ½ x 8, 0-7818-0178-8
$9.95 pb (199)

DICTIONARY OF 1000 FRENCH PROVERBS
edited by Peter Mertvago
131 pages, 5 x 7, 0-7818-0400-0
$11.95 pb (146)

TREASURY OF FRENCH LOVE PO[...]
PROVERBS IN FRENCH AND ENGL[...]
edited and translated by Richard Brany[...]
A bilingual gift collection of popular F[...]
centuries. Works from Baudelaire, Hu[...]
into the French perspective on roman[...]
128 pages, 5 x 7, 0-7818-0359-4
$11.95 hc (580)
Audiobook: 0-7818-0360-8
$12.95 (577)

500 FRENCH WORDS AND PHRASES FOR CHIL[...]
written and edited by Carol Watson and Philippa Moyle
This book used colorful cartoons to teach children basic French phras[...]
and vocabulary.
32 pages, 8 x 10, full color illustrations
0-7818-0267-9
$8.95 (37)

LANGUAGE & TRAVEL GUIDE TO FRANCE
by Elaine Hein
320 pages, 5 ½ x 8 ½
0-7818-0080-30
$14.95 pb (386)

(All prices subject to change.)
TO PURCHASE HIPPOCRENE BOOKS contact your local
bookstore, call (718) 454-2366, or write: HIPPOCRENE BOOKS, 171
Madison Avenue, New York, NY 10016. Please enclose check or credit
card information, adding $5.00 shipping (UPS) for the first book and
$.50 for each additional book.

French Language Titles
from Hippocrene . . .

MASTERING FRENCH
by E.J. Neather
A useful tool for language learning, this method combines a full-size text with two audio cassettes allowing learners to hear proper pronunciation by native speakers as they study the book.
Book: 288 pages, 5 ½ x 8 ½, 0-87052-055-5
$11.95pb (511)
2 Cassettes: 0-87052-060-1
$12.95 (512)

MASTERING ADVANCED FRENCH
by E.J. Neather
An advanced course of French utilizing the method of *Mastering French..*
Book: 278 pages, 5 ½ x 8 ½, 0-7818-0312-8
$14.95 pb (41)
2 Cassettes; 0-7818-0313-6
$12.95 (54)

FRENCH HANDY DICTIONARY
For the traveler of independent spirit and curious mind, this practical dictionary will help you to communicate, not just get by. Common phrases are conveniently listed through key words. Pronunciation follows each entry and a reference section reviews all major grammar points.
120 pages, 5 x 8 , 0-7818-0010-2
$8.95 pb (155)

FRENCH-ENGLISH/ENGLISH-FRENCH
PRACTICAL DICTIONARY With Larger Print
by Rosalind Williams
35,000 entries, 386 pages, 5 ½ x 8, 0-7818-0178-8
$9.95 pb (199)

DICTIONARY OF 1000 FRENCH PROVERBS
edited by Peter Mertvago
131 pages, 5 x 7, 0-7818-0400-0
$11.95 pb (146)

TREASURY OF FRENCH LOVE POEMS, QUOTATIONS AND PROVERBS IN FRENCH AND ENGLISH
edited and translated by Richard Branyon
A bilingual gift collection of popular French love poems, spanning eight centuries. Works from Baudelaire, Hugo, Rimbaud and others offer insight into the French perspective on romance.
128 pages, 5 x 7, 0-7818-0359-4
$11.95 hc (580)
Audiobook: 0-7818-0360-8
$12.95 (577)

500 FRENCH WORDS AND PHRASES FOR CHILDREN
written and edited by Carol Watson and Philippa Moyle
This book used colorful cartoons to teach children basic French phrases and vocabulary.
32 pages, 8 x 10, full color illustrations
0-7818-0267-9
$8.95 (37)

LANGUAGE & TRAVEL GUIDE TO FRANCE
by Elaine Hein
320 pages, 5 ½ x 8 ½
0-7818-0080-30
$14.95 pb (386)

(All prices subject to change.)
TO PURCHASE HIPPOCRENE BOOKS contact your local bookstore, call (718) 454-2366, or write: HIPPOCRENE BOOKS, 171 Madison Avenue, New York, NY 10016. Please enclose check or credit card information, adding $5.00 shipping (UPS) for the first book and $.50 for each additional book.